"You Want Me, Too, Don't You?"

Kaler slowly brushed the curve of her jaw with his thumb as his gaze roamed her face.

"I don't even know you anymore," Leigh said.

"You don't have to know me to want me. You wanted me that first day in my office, and you didn't know me then."

"That's not true."

"A guy like me learns to read people's eyes real quick. I saw what was in yours that day. A little fear, the usual female wariness and a whole lot of sexual fascination."

She raised her eyes and looked into his face. "You weren't like any man I'd ever met. Maybe that's why I couldn't seem to make my usual defenses work against you."

Part of the night seemed trapped in his eyes as he stared down at her. "I never had any defenses at all against you. That's what scared me. It still does."

Dear Reader,

Welcome to Silhouette Desire! The fabulous things we have to offer you in Silhouette Desire just keep on coming. October is simply chock-full of delicious goodies to keep even the most picky romance reader happy all month long.

First, we have a thrilling new *Man of the Month* book from talented author Paula Detmer Riggs. It's called *A Man of Honor,* and I know Max Kaler is a hero you'll never forget.

Next, Annette Broadrick's SONS OF TEXAS series continues with *Courtship Texas Style!* Please *don't* worry if you didn't catch the beginning of this series, because each of the SONS OF TEXAS stands alone (and how!).

For those of you who are Lass Small fans—and you all know who you are!—her connecting series about those FABULOUS BROWN BROTHERS continues with *Two Halves.* Again, please don't fret if you haven't read about the *other* Brown Brothers, because Mike Brown is a hero in his own right!

I'm always thrilled to be able to introduce new authors to the Silhouette Desire family, and Anne Marie Winston is someone you'll be seeing a lot of in the future. Her first published book ever, *Best Kept Secrets,* is highlighted this month as a PREMIERE title. Watch for future Desire books by this talented newcomer in Spring 1993.

This month is completed in a most delightful way with Jackie Merritt's *Black Creek Ranch* (a new book by Jackie is always a thrill) and Donna Carlisle's *It's Only Make Believe.*

As for November... well, I'd tell you all about it, but I've run out of space. You'll just have to wait!

So until next month, happy reading,

Lucia Macro
Senior Editor

PAULA
DETMER RIGGS

A MAN OF HONOR

SILHOUETTE *Desire*

Published by Silhouette Books New York

America's Publisher of Contemporary Romance

SILHOUETTE BOOKS
300 East 42nd St., New York, N.Y. 10017

A MAN OF HONOR

Copyright © 1992 by Paula Detmer Riggs

All rights reserved. Except for use in any review,
the reproduction or utilization of this work in
whole or in part in any form by any electronic,
mechanical or other means, now known or
hereafter invented, including xerography,
photocopying and recording, or in any information
storage or retrieval system, is forbidden without
the permission of the publisher, Silhouette Books,
300 E. 42nd St., New York, N.Y. 10017

ISBN: 0-373-05744-X

First Silhouette Books printing October 1992

All the characters in this book have no existence
outside the imagination of the author and have
no relation whatsoever to anyone bearing the same
name or names. They are not even distantly
inspired by any individual known or unknown
to the author, and all incidents are pure invention.

® and ™: Trademarks used with authorization.
Trademarks indicated with ® are registered
in the United States Patent and Trademark Office,
the Canada Trade Mark Office and in
other countries.

Printed in the U.S.A.

Books by Paula Detmer Riggs

Silhouette Intimate Moments

Beautiful Dreamer #183
Fantasy Man #226
Suspicious Minds #250
Desperate Measures #283
Full Circle #303
Tender Offer #314
A Lasting Promise #344
Forgotten Dream #364
Paroled! #440

Silhouette Desire

Rough Passage #633
A Man of Honor #744

Silhouette Books

Silhouette Summer Sizzlers 1992
"Night of the Dark Moon"

PAULA DETMER RIGGS

discovers material for her writing in her varied life experiences. During her first five years of marriage to a naval officer, she lived in nineteen different locations on the West Coast, gaining familiarity with places as diverse as San Diego and Seattle. While working at a historical site in San Diego, she wrote, directed and narrated fashion shows and became fascinated with the early history of California.

She writes romances because "I think we all need an escape from the high-tech pressures that face us every day, and I believe in happy endings. Isn't that why we keep trying, in spite of all the roadblocks and disappointments along the way?"

For my son, Alex, and all the other heroes in the state of Washington

One

<hr>

Summer days started early in Washington's Wenatchee Valley. Orchardists needed to be in the fields early, before the wind had a chance to rise, and in the giant warehouses where the pears and apples were kept in cold storage, the packers liked to get a fast start on the day.

In the old railroad town of Cashmere, the Orchard Café was already packed, and it wasn't yet seven. The men hunched over the steaming plates worried more about hail damage and apple borers and pear-blight than their latest cholesterol count. As always, their conversation was lively and liberally spiced with rough obscenities ignored by the women worrying aloud about children and unemployment and stretching each paycheck to the maximum.

One man sat alone in a corner booth. Maximillian Kaler was neither a packer nor an orchardist, although he'd done both in his forty-seven years.

Because the day promised to be another mid-August scorcher, he was wearing a bloodred tank top and khaki shorts with his well-broken-in hiking boots and thick wool socks.

More at home outdoors than inside, he was deeply tanned, and the soft blond hair curling over the shirt's neckline looked almost white.

The same sun that had bronzed his face had bleached his hair straw gold and tipped the lashes framing his deep-set blue eyes with the same metallic glint.

At a shade under six feet, he wasn't unusually tall in an area that had bred loggers for generations, but his wide shoulders and deep chest made even the largest man think twice about taking him on in a fight, fair or otherwise.

"Heard you were due back yesterday, Kale."

Belle Steinert's ruddy, hausfrau face crinkled into a motherly smile as she slid a heavily laden plate of kraut, sausage and potato pancakes in front of him.

Admitting to sixty, but closer to seventy, Belle had owned the Orchard Café for as long as Kaler could remember. She'd even learned to cook under Attila the Hun, some of her more browbeaten customers claimed behind her back.

Kaler was used to her gruff words and bossy way, even found them soothing when he was feeling more alone than usual. Maybe that was why, as a kid, he'd spent more time in Belle's home than his own.

In those days, the shack on Boomer's Ridge where he'd grown up had been overrun with toddlers and babies and the constant bickering of his overworked parents. In Belle's clapboard rambler he could always find a quiet place to read and enough food to satisfy his always enormous appetite.

She alone of the people who remembered him and his family knew why he'd come home to the Wenatchee Valley after an absence of twenty-three years. And she alone had seen him try to drink himself to death before he'd found the guts to put his shame and regret behind him and get on with his life.

Now he made as good a living as he needed leading backpackers and fishermen into the wildly beautiful, treacherous lands of the eastern Cascades. Life was hard in the valley, but it was also liberating, and he had the kind of freedom most men would kill for. Every day he told himself he should be grateful.

"Retired," it said in his personnel jacket at U.S. Customs headquarters in Washington, D.C. Most of his buddies thought he'd been damn lucky not to end up in a cell for years.

Yeah, he was lucky, all right.

Here's to freedom, he thought as he lifted his icy beer mug to his mouth. The ale was strong and bitter, just the way he liked it. But it was also the first alcohol he'd had in two weeks, and it hit his empty stomach like a rush of adrenaline.

He sucked in hard and waited for the queasiness to pass. Beer and sauerkraut for breakfast. Once it had been tortillas and tequila, but that had been in another place and another lifetime.

"Where'd you take the tourists this time?" Belle asked as she slipped into the booth to rest her tired feet for a few precious minutes.

"Granite Lake." He put down his beer and picked up his fork. Until yesterday, he'd been baby-sitting a party of rich Seattle accountants on a fishing excursion to one of the Cascades' most remote areas.

"Took us five days to get there with the four of them bragging the whole time on how many fish they were planning to catch," he said between bites of kraut.

"Before they even wet a line, they'd polished off the case of bourbon they'd hidden in their packs, and I had to catch the fish to feed them for the three days it took to get over their damn hangovers. By then it was time to start back. They never did catch a fish."

Belle chuckled. "Sounds like 'coasters.' They talk big, but there's not much muscle under the talk."

Kaler allowed himself a grin. It felt a tad rusty but genuine enough. "I've been thinking of taking the fall off this year, maybe fix the roof on the old place and clean up the old orchard. Might even put in a few trees next spring."

Belle shook her head, setting her snowy curls to bobbing. "If you're going to take time off, why don't you spend it someplace warm, like one of those South Sea islands they're always showing on TV?"

"I'm trying to get away from the tourists, not be one." He savored another mouthful of kraut and sausage before washing it down with a long swallow of ale.

"You spend too much time alone as it is. Only time you come to town is for some of my potato cakes."

"A man has his vices, sure enough."

Leaning back, he reached into the pocket of his shirt for the one cigar he allowed himself a day and clamped it between his teeth. Before he could reach for a match, however, Belle plucked it free and tucked it into the pocket of her spotless apron.

"Hey, I need that!" he protested, then scowled at the rumble of laughter from four apple growers at the next table.

"Watch out, Kale," one of growers called out. "Before you know it, she'll bully you into wearin' ties and shavin' every day."

"The hell she will," Kaler called back, his dark blue eyes turning mulish as they challenged Belle's lighter pair.

He saw the determined glint there and sighed inwardly. Sure enough, she leaned forward and brushed his coarse, straw-gold hair away from his broad forehead, something she'd been doing regularly since he was five. As far as he knew, she'd never been pleased with the result.

Resigned to indulging her one more time, he tried to ignore the amused looks he was getting from others who were subjected to the same periodic fussing.

"Man and boy, you always did need tending," Belle announced with a motherly cluck of her tongue as she settled into her seat again. "It's past time you found yourself a nice, understanding woman to smooth out that grumpy disposition of yours."

Kaler wondered if he could sneak the cigar out of her pocket before she slugged him. "Women don't smooth a man's bad disposition. They cause it."

"Maybe you just haven't found the right one."

"Maybe I'm not looking, either." Sooner or later, most wanted more than he cared to give. Commitment. Permanence. Romance. The words were sometimes different. The meaning was the same. Sooner or later, a woman wanted love.

So had he. Once.

As a kid he'd been tongue-tied around the girls in his class, and as a teenager he'd been too busy putting food on the table to care much about dating. At the time, his five younger sisters had warned him that he would fall hard when he fell. They'd been right.

He'd been thirty-five and battered around the edges. Love had taken him by surprise, but, like most things that took his interest, he'd given all that he had. When it ended, he'd been shell-shocked for a long time. He still carried the scars inside, where no one could see.

The door to Main Street opened, and two men in work clothes and dirty "gimme" caps entered, accompanied by the tinkling of the bell over the door.

"Got steak and apple fritters this morning," Belle called as they headed toward the only two stools available at the counter.

"You got that every morning," the taller of the two complained before giving Kaler a friendly nod.

"Mornin', Kale."

"Morning, Fred. Karl."

Both men, longtime growers in the valley, had been cheated at one time or another by Kaler's father, Patrick, but they had come to accept his oldest son as a man of his word. And, in recent years, the best shot in Chelan County.

"Heard you said yes to Jerry Hanson over to the co-op 'bout that little job," the man named Karl said grimly as he paused by Kaler's booth. "Good luck to you."

Fred grunted his agreement. "Shoot first and don't take no chances."

"Don't worry," Kaler returned dryly. "I know the odds."

"Know you do. That don't mean it'll be easy." With that, the two men continued toward the counter.

"So it's true, what I been hearing," Belle accused in a low voice when they were out of earshot.

"Depends on what you've been hearing."

"I heard you might be going back out today," Belle persisted. "With that old Winchester of yours and a kill permit from Fish and Game."

He shrugged. "I had some free time."

Belle snorted. "Don't give me that. If you had free time, it's because you *made* time. And you made time because no one else was willing to take the job."

She edged out of the booth, then glanced pointedly at the folded newspaper he'd brought with him but hadn't yet opened. "There's already two people in the hospital over to Wenatchee. Don't you dare be number three, you hear me?"

"Yes, ma'am."

Belle swatted at his unshaven cheek, and he ducked, taking the blow on his thick forearm. His rumbling boyish laugh surprised them both.

"You might have everyone else up here intimidated, but not me, Max Kaler. I know what a softie you are inside."

"I just let you think that so you'll fix me kraut and potato pancakes for breakfast."

Belle chuckled. "I'll be back with your coffee after I make a fresh pot," she promised, but her world-weary eyes remained clouded with concern as she headed toward the kitchen.

Kaler watched her with softened eyes few had ever seen, until he remembered where he was and picked up his fork again.

He hadn't allowed many women to bully him in his life. His mother had been one. Belle was another. He never let himself think about the third.

Absently rubbing two fingers across the thin white scar above his right eye, he thought about the night he'd lain in the gutter outside this place, bleeding from the gash he'd put in his head when he passed out drunk before he could get to Belle's door.

It had taken him a long time to live that down, and an even longer time rebuilding the respect of his neighbors. He still had trouble respecting himself.

Forcing his mind away from the past, he flipped open his newspaper to read while he ate, a habit he'd developed after he'd quit school at twelve to help out in the family orchard. He was almost finished with the first section when he realized he wasn't alone.

He looked up, expecting to find Belle and her ubiquitous coffeepot. Instead, the small, dark-haired woman standing with one hand on the back of the seat opposite was meticulously dressed in linen and silk.

Years of discipline kept his expression impassive, but Kaler felt the muscles of his spine turning slab hard. For a long, terrible moment he wondered if the woman standing like a glossy magazine photo in front of him had walked out of one of his dreams to taunt him.

Her name was Henrietta Elisabeth Leigh Bradbury. He'd called her Leigh in the office and Hank in bed.

The day had hardly begun, and yet she radiated energy and freshness, from the top of her lustrous brown hair to the tips of her stylish Italian pumps. Even her profile, as delicate as a pricey antique cameo, suggested generations of refined breeding and genteel rearing. Anything less would be unthinkable. After all, she had come from a very long line of aristocratic Southern belles.

Class and steely determination to succeed, that was Leigh.

Kaler leaned back against the slick vinyl covering on the booth's hard seat and extended one arm along the back. "Now I've seen everything," he drawled. "Leigh Bradbury in a place like Belle's. You must be lost."

Her gaze wavered momentarily before she smiled. Only someone who knew her well would notice the ever-so-faint quiver of her smile. He allowed himself a moment of curiosity before ruthlessly casting it aside.

"Not lost. I came looking for you." She cast a quick look around before glancing at the seat across from him. "Is this seat taken?"

"Depends on what you have in mind."

"Talk, Kaler. Just a few minutes of conversation."

"Sorry. I'm fresh out of small talk." He picked up his fork and resumed eating.

"Five minutes shouldn't strain you too much."

Two bites later, he realized that his appetite had disappeared. The potato pancakes that were one of his addictions suddenly tasted like cardboard. Because Leigh was watching him, however, he made himself take a few more bites before putting down his fork again.

Without waiting for an invitation, she slid into the booth and tossed her soft suede bag onto the seat next to her. He caught a whiff of something elusive and French. He'd never known the name, and he'd never known anyone else who'd worn it. Behind each small, sexy ear. In the hollow of her throat. Dabbed on the sensitive skin behind her knees.

After they'd made love, he'd been able to smell the rich, provocative scent on his skin before she'd soaped it away in the shower they'd invariably shared.

Remembering, he had to take a moment to work through the instant reaction. His head told him he no longer wanted this woman. His body knew otherwise.

"So... how are you, Kaler?"

"I'm making it okay."

"So I've heard."

She seemed to be looking him over with frank curiosity, and he felt a stirring under his skin wherever her gaze touched. Did she remember the first time those sloe-brown eyes had seen all of him? What would she say if he asked? he wondered.

Something diplomatic and clever that would leave him groping for an answer, no doubt. But then, he'd never been a match for her when it came to words. No way could a self-educated marine grunt best a summa cum laude master's graduate from Georgetown. Once he'd thought it didn't matter. Now he knew better.

"Don't tell me you came all the way up here from Phoenix just to ask questions about me?" The slow arching of his eyebrow elicited a brief curve of her lips.

"I won't. And I didn't."

He drained his mug and pushed it aside. He was tempted to break his long-standing rule and order another. "I'd heard you got married," he said, stretching his long legs away from hers. "Congratulations."

"Edward died two years ago."

A shadow dimmed some of the soft luster of her eyes. He didn't allow his surprise to show. Nor the swift tug of sympathy that took him unaware. "Sorry."

"So am I."

Sun streamed through the large front window, touching her face with gold and highlighting the freckles only partially hidden by the lightest of makeup. There were nineteen. He'd counted them once, with his tongue.

"Up here on vacation, I imagine," he said with just enough sarcasm in his voice to erase the sadness in her eyes.

"You still get right to the point, don't you?"

"Saves time that way."

Once upon a time his mama would have turned his butt red for speaking to a lady with such discourtesy. Now he told himself he didn't care.

"I came because I need your help—as a guide."

"I'm booked."

"I'll pay what you would earn. More. Name your price."

His fingers closed around his coffee cup. He'd never hit a woman. Never would. "I'm not for sale."

"As a favor, then." Her eyes pleaded with him. It was the same beseeching, vulnerable expression he'd carried away with him when he'd walked out on her. The same expression that had haunted his drunken days and nights for so long.

"For old times' sake, you mean?"

From the corner of his eye, Kaler saw Belle emerge from the kitchen, throw him a quick double take and then make a beeline for his booth, pad in hand.

"Can I get you something, miss?" she asked Leigh politely.

"I'd love a cup of coffee."

"Got a fresh pot brewing right now. Won't be but a minute." Belle paused, her expression expectant. When no one spoke, she cleared her throat to ask, "You take cream and sugar?"

"Black, please."

Nodding, Belle darted Kaler a speculative look. He groaned inwardly. Sooner or later, he was in for a grilling. Good thing he was heading into the mountains. Not even Belle would dare follow him there.

"Anything else I can get you folks? Another menu, maybe?"

Kaler narrowed his gaze to warn her off. "Just the coffee."

"Comin' right up, *Mr.* Kaler, sir."

Belle's impudent grin had him grinding his back teeth. By noon it would be all over the valley that he'd allowed a lady "coaster" to share his booth.

"Looks like you're still winning friends and influencing people," Leigh murmured when Belle had once again disappeared behind the swinging door.

"Like I once told you, what you see is what you get. You didn't believe me then, as I remember. Wanted to make me into some kind of by-the-book bureaucrat instead of a guy doing his job the best way he knew how."

Leigh's eyes flashed gold, the first chink in the seamlessly smooth wall of her composure. "You don't intend to make this easy, do you?"

"Any reason why I should?"

"As you said, for old times' sake."

He reached for his cigar, then remembered seeing it disappear into Belle's apron pocket. Sitting back, he allowed himself a small tight smile. "In case you've forgotten, I don't work for the government any longer and you're not my boss."

"Damn it, Kaler," she grated on a rush of breath that made her breasts push against her thin silk shirt. "I had no choice! How many times do I have to tell you that?"

To his surprise, his own temper was suddenly threatening. "You had a choice, and you made it!"

"You told Mendoza you would kill him if he didn't turn informer," she said heatedly. "What was I supposed to do when I found out, let you go ahead and slaughter a prisoner?"

"I let him *think* he would die. I never said I would be the one pulling the trigger."

"You admitted that you were going to turn him loose and tell his buddies where to find him if he didn't talk.

'One bloody worthless courier in exchange for a message Mendoza's buddies couldn't ignore,' I think was how you put it.''

Kaler felt the quick burn of frustration on his face. "Mendoza was scum."

"He was also your prisoner, entitled by law to your protection. Deliberately getting a man murdered was a clear violation of those rights, don't you think?"

"Yeah, but it didn't happen, did it? And Mendoza turned out to be a human Rolodex. Because I bent those damn rules you're so fond of quoting, a lot a bad guys are now long-term guests in federal prison."

She shot him a pitying look that had his back teeth all but welded together. "The ends justify the means, right?"

"Damn straight it does! In case you haven't figured it out yet, Ms. Georgetown Phi Beta Kappa, we're fighting a war out there, a war we're losing. Way I was taught, there aren't any rules in war except staying alive to win."

"That doesn't mean we have to sink to the level of the very people we're trying to stop."

"Pardon me all to hell, Ms. Bradbury, ma'am. We wouldn't want you to get those lily-white hands of yours all smeared with blood. No sirree, ma'am."

His fist hit the table with enough impact to slosh the remains of his first cup of coffee onto the table. Conversation ceased abruptly, as though someone had fired a shot into the ceiling.

Suddenly Kaler noticed the silence and saw the shocked faces ringing them. He felt his eyes ice over and his mouth thin.

"Show's over," he grated, his eyes cold. At that same moment Belle came hurrying to the table with a cup in one hand and a full pot of coffee in the other.

"You two know each other?" she asked as she refilled Kaler's cup.

"Belle Steinert, meet Leigh Bradbury. Ms. Bradbury here was my boss."

Belle's smile was benignly maternal, the kind of smile that invited confidences. "That a fact?"

Kaler remained silent, forcing Leigh to answer. "Actually, no one ever really bosses Kaler." Leigh drew her cup closer. She'd done that often in the past, made some little movement or gesture to buy her time to frame her answer.

He rested his forearm on the table and waited. Belle glanced from one to the other. Holding her breath, no doubt, Kaler thought. The place could burn down around her before she would miss out on this little tidbit.

Leigh took a dainty sip before gracing Belle with a polite smile. "Kaler was almost a legend in the customs service. I'd heard all about him before I even met him. Everyone in my training class wanted to be assigned to the Southwest District, just so they could work for him." With slow deliberation, her gaze sought his.

"'Kaler's the best'," they told us during training. "'Do what he does and you can't go wrong'."

A man who didn't know better would swear there was a sheen of tears in her dark brown eyes. A man who believed that was heading for a load of hurt.

"Yeah, well, nobody thinks that now, thanks to you."

"Seems like you two have some unfinished business," Belle said as she looked from one to the other.

Kaler got to his feet and threw a handful of bills onto the table. "Not me," he said with a curt nod. "I'm done here." He nodded to Belle, retrieved his straw Stetson from the seat next to him and left, banging the door behind him.

Leigh exhaled slowly, cold, in spite of the café's stuffy heat. She sensed the sympathy of Belle and the others in the room and stiffened her shoulders.

Her mother would be proud of her, she thought numbly as she curved her lips in a polite smile for the older woman with the kind eyes. Outer serenity in the midst of calamity, a mark of a true lady.

"I don't know why I thought it would be easy," Leigh said as other conversations resumed around her.

Belle slipped into the spot Kaler had just vacated and regarded Leigh with undisguised sympathy. "At least you put some fire in his belly, honey. Nobody's been able to do that for Kale since he came back here seven years ago."

Leigh folded her hands neatly in her lap. Too bad her stomach hadn't learned to fake calmness the way her face had, she thought. At the moment it was doing wild loop-the-loops beneath the snug waistband of her best linen skirt.

"I'd forgotten how fierce he could be when he's cornered."

"Kale hasn't forgotten a thing," Belle murmured softly. "Sometimes I think he uses his memories to lash himself raw and bleeding whenever he starts thinking about liking himself again."

Leigh studied the woman's plump, homely face, searching for signs of censure, but she saw only compassion and sorrow. "I . . . Do you know Kaler well?"

"'Bout as well as he lets anyone know him."

The woman's smile was strangely knowing. For an obviously curious woman, she was asking remarkably few questions. "He's told you about me, hasn't he?" Leigh asked softly.

Belle nodded. "More than he thinks he has."

"Then you know I'm the one who recommended his dismissal from Customs after fifteen years of near-perfect service."

"Way I heard it, he didn't give you much choice."

"I could have called Mendoza a liar when he and his lawyer brought those charges against Kaler. Maybe I should have."

There were plenty of her colleagues who thought she should have been the one railroaded out. Next to Kaler's record, hers was anemic at best.

She'd been an expert shot on the range, but his skills had been learned in the Marine Corps when he was only seventeen, then tested in the kind of dirty, bloody combat he'd never wanted to talk about, even with her.

Her training had taught her first-aid skills and lifesaving techniques, but Kaler had been the one who'd used safety pins to keep a gut-shot youngster's belly intact until he could get him to the nearest aid station.

He'd also bullied and protected and more than once saved the life of some green trainee outmatched and outgunned by the ruthless, amoral *coyotes* and drug traffickers running the Mexican border.

He'd been the best, the rarest of the rare—a man who was truly making the world a better place. His courage, his intelligence, his deeply genuine caring—they had been the benchmarks by which she'd judged all other men and invariably found them wanting. Then, with one disastrous decision, one lapse of honor, one flaw in judgment, he had spoiled everything.

"Is there some reason in particular you came looking for Kale after seven years?" Belle asked, redirecting Leigh's thoughts instantly.

"I need him," she said, then realized exactly what she'd said. "That is, I need a favor. My father is camping near here, and I have to find him before...well, it's a sort of medical emergency."

"Serious?"

"Serious enough. Father had a routine physical before he left Virginia on this vacation. Some last-minute test results just came in the day before yesterday, and Father's doctor discovered an aneurysm in one of the vessels of his heart. When Dr. MaCallister couldn't reach Father, he called me. When I told him where Father had gone, he decided the risk was great enough to warrant his breaking professional confidentiality. I caught the first available flight from Phoenix."

Leigh saw sympathy flash across Belle's face, and for the first time in forty-eight hours of constant worry and activity, she didn't feel quite so alone and scared.

"Dr. Mac said that I absolutely have to get Father to a hospital as quickly as possible for surgery. Everyone I've talked to in this area has recommended Kaler as the best man to find him, wherever he is."

"Give him some time, honey. He can be grumpy as a spring-hungry grizzly but he'll come 'round."

"That's just it, Mrs. Steinert! I don't have any more time. Dr. Mac said that high altitude is the worst possible thing for a man with Father's condition." Leigh glanced at the coffee cooling in the cup.

"Go ahead, honey. Take a sip. Pardon me for saying so, but you look like you could use the caffeine."

"I've been up since three," Leigh admitted. And driving the road from Seattle since four she thought. Eyes sharp as any eagle's watched Leigh closely as she politely managed a few sips.

"Better have another taste," Belle insisted when Leigh would have pushed the cup away. "You need more color in that pretty face of yours."

Summoning what little composure she had left, Leigh chugged down the rest of the cup's contents without gagging and then immediately thought of Mama Sarah, her nanny. Mama Sarah and Belle Steinert were a lot alike. Impossible bullies, both of them, and chock-full of motherly love.

"Feeling more perky now?"

"Yes, thanks." Leigh snuck a look at her watch. Seven-thirty. Now what? she thought. Go after Kaler or try to find someone else? It was on the tip of her tongue to ask Belle's advice when the pimply-faced busboy dropped a tray full of dirty dishes, spattering the floor with glass and cold coffee.

"Darn Wilhelm," Belle muttered over the buzz of comment. "Tries to do too much too fast." She inhaled deeply, then refocused her shrewd gaze on Leigh's face.

"Tell Kale about your father. He'll help you."

Leigh let her doubts show in her eyes. "I was just about to ask you if you could recommend someone else."

"Let me tell you a little story about my friend Kale. About ten years back I had a fire and no insurance. Started back there in the kitchen. Wiped me out financially. I had creditors banging on my door at all hours, about to hound me to death. Kale was living in Phoenix then, but one of his sisters wrote and told him about my troubles. Next thing I know, there's a cashier's check for thirty thousand dollars sliding through my mail slot."

"From Kaler?"

"Yep."

The Porsche, Leigh thought. The one Kaler had babied and pampered as though it were his only child. He'd all but mounted an armed guard to prevent dings and dust. And then, one day, it had disappeared, replaced by an old World War Two jeep from the junkyard. Easier on the insurance premiums, he'd told her with a shrug when she'd questioned him.

"There was a note, too," Belle added. "Said he'd had a windfall and wouldn't miss the money. Wouldn't even take my note. Still won't, and you know why?"

Leigh shook her head. "Because money isn't important to Kale, not the way it's important to most folks who grow up dirt-poor the way he did. Friends are important to him. He don't have that many, but he keeps the ones he has."

Leigh inhaled slowly. "Kaler never talked much about Cashmere or the people here. I had the feeling he didn't have too many pleasant memories."

"He was doing a man's work at twelve and was head of a family of eight when he was fifteen. Through it all, he never lost his sense of humor or gave up trying to make things better. He was also one of the most purely honorable people I'd ever met, but then, that's what got him into trouble, wasn't it? The fact that he wouldn't lie to you or anyone else about what he did?"

Eyes downcast, Leigh ran her nail over a scratch in the wooden tabletop. "But he lied to Mendoza, Mrs. Steinert. How can that be honorable?"

Belle's gaze sharpened. "I gather he never told you about his brother Andy, either?"

Leigh took a moment to adjust to the abrupt change of subject. She was coming to understand Belle now. Like Mama Sarah, the more important the destination, the longer she took to get there.

"Just that he was killed in the Vietnam War."

"Not *in* the war. Kale was already serving overseas when Andy joined up, so the Marine Corps couldn't send him to Vietnam right away. Some kind of military law or something." Her eyebrows lifted like two fuzzy white caterpillars, and Leigh nodded.

"Andy was the one Kaler loved best of all his brothers and sisters, probably because the kid wasn't quite as bright as he should be. Not that he was retarded, mind you, but it took him longer than most to learn. Not like Kale. Tell him something once and he remembers it forever."

"What happened?"

Belle remained thoughtful, her blue eyes brooding and sad. "Andy was stationed down in San Diego when he died. Heroin overdose, the medics said. He was only nineteen."

Leigh thought about the wrapped coil tightness in Kaler's face whenever he mentioned his youngest brother, which hadn't been all that often, and her churning stomach dropped like a fast elevator.

"He never talked much about either of his brothers, or about his sisters, for that matter."

"Kale quit the marines right after that, and next thing I heard, he was working down on the border for the customs service, doing some kind of undercover drug work. Swore he'd spend the rest of his life making sure what happened to Andy never happened to somebody else's brother. Heard he'd almost died trying to do just that."

Leigh stared straight ahead. "He'd just gotten out of the hospital when I met him. His cover had been blown, and he'd been wounded, but he'd made the arrest and been promoted to district supervisor." For some reason Leigh's vision was blurring whenever she tried to focus on Belle's sympathetic blue eyes. She hesitated, then added stiffly, "Actually, he was my boss for a long time before I was his. And even then, that was only because I had a degree and he didn't. I would have been furious, but Kaler understood. It was the system, he said."

Belle nodded. "When Kale brought Andy home to be buried next to his mama, I've never seen a man grieve so hard. That is, until he came home seven years ago. Guess I understand why now. You two were in love, weren't you?"

"I was. I thought Kaler was, too, although he never said so." He'd asked her to live with him, though, and, later, to marry him. She'd turned him down, not because she hadn't loved him, but because spouses couldn't work together. And she loved her job almost as much as she loved Kaler.

"Don't look so sad, honey. Take it from an old woman who's had herself two good men in her life. A man will forgive a woman anything if he loves her."

"But that's the problem, isn't it?" Leigh cleared her throat and said politely, "I, um, thank you for the coffee and the shoulder to cry on, Mrs. Steinert. I understand a lot of things now," she said as she concentrated on gathering up her purse. Most of all she realized now that Kaler had never trusted her enough to share his pain with her. Only his pleasure.

"Name's Belle, and you're most welcome." Belle patted Leigh's hand in motherly comfort. "If you're going after Kale, you'd best hurry. He doesn't stay put long."

"I'm going after him," Leigh said as she slid from the booth. She had come too far to back off now, not when her father's life might be at stake.

Kaler was a man of careful habits. Too many good men had been killed because of a moment's oversight or carelessness.

His trail gear was the best he could find. Each piece, from the utilitarian two-man tent to the lightweight canteen to the watertight first-aid kit, was checked and double-checked for damage and wear after every trip. Nothing was ever put away unless it had been cleaned, repaired if necessary, and was ready for use at a middle-of-the-night's notice.

His rifle was always loaded and kept close at hand. A few years older than he was, it was a vintage Winchester caliber 30-06 with a hand-carved walnut stock and sights he'd customized himself. Forty-one summers ago his father had taught him to hunt with that same rifle—not for sport, but for food. There had been some weeks when Kaler had been solely responsible for putting meat on the table.

Times had been hard then. Hell, when hadn't they been? Patrick Kaler had had an Irishman's love of drink and a reckless man's disregard for self-control. As a consequence, Kaler was the eldest of eight children, older by some three years than his oldest sister, Essie.

Hunger had been a powerful motivator, especially for a gangly, hyperactive kid who'd outgrown his clothes every few months. After the first few weeks, he'd learned quickly never to miss. At seven, he'd already mastered life's basic lesson—get the job done, no matter what it took.

A mountain jay scolded him impatiently from the top of a gnarled pear tree as Kaler hefted his fully loaded backpack into the Jeep and fastened down the recently repaired canvas top.

By dusk he would be deep in the thick growth of towering pines. By nightfall he would be lying in his bedroll, watching the stars and savoring the familiar sounds of the forest.

He figured a week at the most to get the job done. Probably less, if he fell into any luck at all. He checked his watch. A few minutes past eight.

Already the sultry lowland heat had coated his skin with a fine layer of sweat. Funny thing about heat, he thought as he slipped his rifle into the clamps holding it upright against the dash. The heat in the jungles of Vietnam had been smothering, the kind that made a man long for a cold beer and deep shade. It had soaked his fatigues and rotted his combat boots. He'd hated it, especially during the long boring weeks when he'd been confined to a bed in a battalion hospital, fighting off a near-fatal infection caused by a shrapnel wound in his thigh.

During his years in the Southwestern U.S., however, he'd come to relish the dry desert heat. At night he'd slept nude, often with the windows thrown wide. To this day he never smelled sagebrush without thinking about those surprisingly cool, silent desert nights, and the pint-sized woman who'd invariably nestled close.

Life had been good then. The best. For the first time since he'd stopped being a little boy and started taking care of an endless stream of babies, he'd felt, well, cherished was as close as he could come to describing the feeling he'd had then.

Kaler closed his eyes and tried to ignore the sick feeling in his belly. Memories were dangerous things. Dangerous because they couldn't be controlled. Dangerous because they often led a man onto treacherous ground.

Never look back, he'd vowed one long ago morning after that long-ago night in Belle's bedroom when his head had been throbbing and his gut had been filled with shame.

Alone and still suffering the sweats and shakes of too many drunken nights and days, he'd finally faced himself and what he'd done. A man had almost died because Max Kaler hadn't been able to live with his own guilt. He'd violated his own principles, broken laws he could have recited verbatim down to the last comma, and for what? His kid brother was still dead, and he'd lost the only woman he'd ever loved.

He wasn't proud of what he'd done, but he couldn't change anything, either. Somehow, somewhere, he had to find the guts to live with the consequences or walk naked into a blizzard the way a disgraced warrior of the Wenatchi tribe had once done.

It hadn't been easy, but he'd managed—until Leigh had plunked her elegant fanny across from him and sent his mind spinning backward over every damn day he'd spent without her.

Kaler kicked the Jeep's front tire and listened for the satisfying thunk of good rubber and optimum pressure. The sun was up on another day, and he had work to do.

Kaler swept off his straw Stetson and finger-combed his shaggy hair before he resettled the hat over his forehead and climbed purposefully into the Jeep's hard bucket seat. Already the canvas upholstery was sticky against his bare legs and the steering wheel was hot to the touch.

The old workhorse engine turned over at the first twist of the key, the result of the hundreds of hours he'd spent during the winter reconditioning the fifty-year-old parts.

Who said newer was better? he thought. He and the Jeep still had a lot of years in them. Good, productive years. His smug grin turned to an impatient scowl. Someone was driving a red Mercedes convertible hell-bent up the rutted lane leading to his place. Dust billowed in its wake, all but obscuring the road from his sight.

Kaler ripped off a string of obscenities as he switched off the motor and slid from the seat. Another two minutes and he would have been long gone.

Seconds later the Mercedes skidded to a stop only a few yards from his Jeep, blocking his escape. The sign on the now-dusty bumper identified it as a rental.

He knew before she stepped from the driver's side that Leigh was at the wheel. The woman had a lead foot and absolute faith in her driving ability.

As she hurried toward him, he noticed that her walk was still graceful, with just a slight hint of sexual promise in the restrained sway of her hips.

Her legs were surprisingly long for such a small-boned woman, and she was enticingly rounded in all the right places. Coltish, she'd laughingly called herself once when he'd set about kissing every sleek inch of her.

"The answer is still no," he said even before she reached him. It didn't stop her. Nothing ever had.

"You promised me five minutes. My time wasn't up when you walked out."

"Look, Leigh, ordinarily I take whatever job comes my way. Why the hell not, right? However, I'm committed to another job. End of discussion."

He turned away, but Leigh slipped past him to block his way. Instinctively she rested her fingertips on his bare forearm. The muscles beneath became steel, rejecting even that light touch.

"It's Father. He's sick, maybe dying. He has an aneurysm in one of the small vessels around his heart. His doctor didn't see it at first and gave him a clean bill of health. Then, two days ago, the results of some additional tests came in. There it was, this little ballooning place."

"Get to the point, Leigh. What's that got to do with me?"

"He's up here, backpacking in the state park above Wenatchee, following something called Icicle Canyon." She frowned. "I...uh, suppose you know where that is?"

Kaler tilted his head and studied the worry lines around her eyes. Like him, she was seven years older. Unlike him, she had improved with age.

"My brother got lost up there once. Took me two days to find him and haul his butt home."

"Don't you see!" she cried. "That's exactly what I need you to do for Father. He needs to be hospitalized as soon as possible so that the aneurysm can be repaired."

"Take my word for it, Leigh. Winston Bradbury's too mean to die." He made a move to walk around her. Once again she moved to block his way.

"Please, Kaler. I know you and Father never got along, but he's a human being, and he might die."

"Think a minute, Leigh. Your father's a prominent man. All you have to do is call the local ranger station and they'll send out a half dozen qualified people to look for him."

"I've already tried them. Unless it's a verified and immediate danger, they don't have the manpower."

The blue jay was back, scolding harshly from the top of the pear tree. Overhead, the first wisps of changing cloud patterns were forming against the bright summer sky, and the air smelled hot. He didn't have time to waste on useless arguing.

"Call Tim Burton at the Chelan County Sheriff's office," he said, with a note of finality.

"He told me to call you."

"Any other time, Leigh, a week from now, even, but I've given my word, and around here, a man who reneges on his word might as well pull up stakes and move away, because he'll never get another day's work."

She looked away, as though to draw strength. When she looked back at him, her lips were ashen. "There's something else you should know. Father isn't alone. He's with a little boy named Daniel. He's my son. If Father should suddenly be taken desperately ill or... or if he should die, Danny would be alone and scared and lost!"

Two hours ago Kaler had been as happy as he'd been in a long time. Now he was fighting a battle with a lot of unwanted feelings and memories, a battle he should have won a long time ago.

"So you were lying when you told me you didn't want children," he said evenly.

Her throat worked smoothly as she swallowed. "No, you were the one who made it very, very clear that you had no intention of taking care of any more children. Seven was enough, you said. Remember?"

How could he forget? He'd been sick to his stomach with nerves when he'd told her. The few women he'd cared enough about to be honest with in the past had given him his walking papers in no uncertain terms. Leigh had been different. He'd been the one getting too serious too fast, and he hadn't wanted to lose her. But he'd also had a need to let her know up front where he stood on the subject of a family.

"You agreed," he reminded her now.

Her eyes grew sad. "I loved you. Being with you was more important to me than having a baby."

It grew very quiet, so quiet that Kaler could hear the rush of blood through the veins in his head. She was right. A child alone in the wilderness wouldn't have much of a chance of surviving for more than a few days without help.

If only he hadn't given Jerry Hanson and the others at the co-op his word. But he had.

"I'll make some calls. I know some guys who used to be on the sheriff's search-and-rescue posse with me before it disbanded a few years back. I'll find you someone good before I go."

"I want you. You're the best. Besides, I...I trust you."

"That's flattering, but it doesn't change things. I can't help you."

Leigh fought a shudder of panic. She'd been so sure, when she told him about Danny...

There was one more card to play. A very dangerous card, one that, once played, could never be withdrawn. Her heart raced, and her hands grew clammy. No, she couldn't do it. Not and live with the consequences.

She closed her eyes and saw her son's mischievous smile and bright blue eyes. *Don't worry, Mommy, I'll take good care of Granddaddy.*

It couldn't be helped, she thought. She would do anything, even risk Kaler's wrath, to keep her boy safe.

"I'm asking you to help me because Daniel is your child, Kaler. I was six weeks pregnant when you walked out."

Two

Thirty years ago, when he'd felt the hot shrapnel slice into his flesh, there had been no pain. It had come later in waves of nearly unbearable agony. He felt that same cold thud now.

"Please, Kaler. Say something. I hate it when you go inside yourself that way."

The expression in his eyes startled her. He seemed almost sad, as though she had tapped a wellspring of grief somewhere deep inside him.

"It could have been the other guy's—your husband."

Leigh hadn't even considered . . . it hadn't even occurred to her, that he might not believe her. The hurt cut deep, leaving a dull throbbing somewhere below her heart.

"I'm telling you it wasn't. If that's not enough there's nothing more I can say."

He walked to the steps and stood staring out at the remnants of the pear orchard where he and his mother had worked day and night just to keep them all fed and clothed and to keep the other kids in school.

"So—I have a son. Six years old."

To Leigh, he sounded less stunned and more disbelieving, arousing a chilly fear. He couldn't turn her down. Not after the terrible chance she'd just taken.

"Actually, he's six and a half. He was a Christmas baby."

A baby, he thought, picturing her heavy with child. His child. The child he'd never allowed himself to want.

"If you want me to beg, I will. Only please, Kaler, say you'll help me. Say you'll help my . . . your . . . son."

He turned to face her. Her features were composed, although her skin seemed to have paled even more. Her eyes, nearly black with emotion, pleaded with him.

Kaler had never had a problem handling the swift barb of an obscene insult or the quick body slam of violence. From the time he was a kid, he'd fought back with all he had—with words or his fists, whichever was appropriate—and he'd fought flat out, no-holds-barred. It was the softer, less familiar emotions that got his tongue tangled in knots and his skin turning fever-clammy.

"You win, Leigh. You've got yourself a guide."

Leigh fought a wave of sickening relief. Her gamble had paid off. "Thank you," she whispered. "Thank you."

"Don't thank me yet. There are conditions."

"Anything."

"I won't take money. Don't offer again."

"I won't."

"If something has happened to your old man and the kid is alone, he'll be scared as hell, in shock, even. I'll need you there to reassure him. You'd better plan to come with me."

Leigh's stomach quivered, but she managed to keep her worry from her tone. "I've already made all the necessary arrangements. My staff doesn't expect me back anytime soon."

"Why did I know that?"

"Danny is my life, Kaler. Nothing can happen to him. It just can't!"

"You'd do anything for him, wouldn't you, Mama Bear?" he said in a low tone. "Even bargain with a man you despise?"

He touched her face, the lightest of touches that only hinted at the power trapped in his lean strong fingers. To see if she would flinch? she wondered as she raised her gaze to his.

"I never despised you, just the things you did."

It wasn't a conscious decision that had him fingering a lock of the soft silky hair framing her face. Tiny beads of perspiration had formed along her hairline, turning the small brown wisps into fragile, vulnerable-looking ringlets.

"Tell me something, Leigh. If you hadn't needed my help, would you ever have told me about the boy?"

She shook her head. "Please don't be upset, Kaler. I...I never told you about Danny because I thought it was for the best."

One of his shaggy wheat-toned eyebrows lifted very slowly. "Best for who? You or me?"

"For...for both of us. And Danny. He thinks my late husband is his father."

Kaler dropped his hand, breaking the connection between them. The set of his hard mouth was familiar, meant to discourage further revelations, but his eyes still held a shadow of that strange sadness.

"No reason for him not to. Right?"

"No, no reason at all."

He glanced at the waiting Jeep before returning his gaze to her face. "Put your gear in the Jeep while I make a couple of calls," he ordered before heading for the porch steps. "You can change inside, if you want. Bathroom's at the end of the hall."

He was already inside his house when Leigh tasted blood and realized that she'd bitten the inside of her lip to keep from begging him to forgive her.

The bone-jarring ride from Cashmere to the trail head at Icicle Creek took several hours. Leigh was stiff and sore by the time Kaler pulled the old Jeep into the parking lot.

"There's Father's car," she said, indicating a silver Jaguar sedan covered by a thick, undisturbed coating of dust. "When I talked to the ranger yesterday, she said he'd taken out a camping permit five days ago."

Kaler swung his Jeep into the next space and killed the engine. The sound of the motor hadn't yet faded before a tall, slender lady ranger was bounding down the wooden steps of the ranger station and heading their way.

"Yo, Kaler!" she called with a cheery wave.

Kaler climbed from the Jeep and pocketed the keys. "Hey, kid, how's it going?" Rusty Friedrickson was red-headed and invariably cheerful, and happily married to a fellow ranger at another state park. She was also a darn fine ranger, one of the best, in Kaler's opinion.

"You made good time," she said after they exchanged friendly hugs.

"Couldn't wait to see that gorgeous bod of yours, babe."

Rusty made a face. "I'll tell Hank you send your respects, you big gorgeous hunk."

Kaler grinned. "When are you gonna wise up and dump that guy?"

"When are you gonna come down from that wild ridge of yours for more than a week at a time?"

Kaler took off his hat and tossed it onto the seat. "Hey, I'm here, aren't I?"

Rusty formed her full lips into an exaggerated pout. "My one chance to have my way with you, and you're with another woman." She turned her attention briefly to Leigh, who was stepping from the Jeep with only a slight wince. "Hello again, Ms. Bradbury!" she called.

Leigh's head was ringing and her thighs felt rubbery after hours of constant tensing. "Hello, yourself. It's good to see you again."

Ranger Friedrickson gave her a sympathetic smile. "You are now one of the privileged few who've been allowed to ride in this old heap." She slapped the Jeep's fender, earning a scowl from the owner. "Hank and I are thinking of forming a survivors' club."

Leigh found herself grinning spontaneously for the first time in forty-eight hours. "Something tells me there aren't that many members."

"You make three."

"Enough insults," Kaler grumbled as he hefted Leigh's pack from the Jeep and leaned it against the heavy steel fender before reaching for his own larger, heavier pack.

Shrugging one shoulder, then the other, to settle the burden more comfortably, he glanced upward toward the wild, dark woods to the west. Ten minutes into those trees, it would be as gloomy as twilight, even on a day as bright as this one.

"How about the chopper?" he asked Rusty as he collected his rifle and locked the Jeep.

"No luck yet, but I've got a call in to headquarters. Fire danger's still low, with more rain predicted. I don't see any reason why the Forest Service can't spare a helicopter for one small mercy mission."

"Did you tell headquarters the guy I'm going after is a former U.S. ambassador?"

"Trust me, Kaler. I gave them the man's entire pedigree."

"I trust you, Rusty. It's the suits in their big offices that give me heartburn." He handed Rusty his car keys as though it were standard practice, before slinging the Winchester over his shoulder.

So this had been one of the calls Kaler had made, Leigh thought. To this lovely, obviously kindhearted ranger who clearly adored him. It wasn't jealousy that raced through her. More like regret, she realized. She had once adored Kaler herself. When he wanted to, the man could be endearingly lovable.

"I wish we could do more to help, but we're short staffed as it is." The ranger sent Leigh an apologetic look.

"It's the same with Customs," Leigh assured her sincerely. "You do what you can with the people you have."

"After Kaler called, I posted a notice at the station asking anyone who saw a boy and an older man to report to the ranger on duty. It's a long shot, but it's something."

"Thank you. I appreciate it."

Leigh reached for her pack, and Rusty rushed to help her struggle into it. "The weatherman is talking about thunderstorms. Try to keep your feet dry, okay?"

"Maybe you'd better put a rush on that chopper, just in case," Leigh said when the pack was settled securely.

Rusty chuckled and pointed to the sky with one thumb. "It'll be ready and waiting by the time Kaler gets all of you back here."

Leigh hesitated, then reached out to give the other woman an awkward hug. ''Thanks, Rusty.''

''Good luck, Leigh.'' Her gaze shifted to Kaler and became grave. ''To both of you.''

Three

———

The moon hadn't yet risen, but the night birds were already flitting from branch to branch. Because the night was warm, Kaler had opted for sleeping under the stars. So had Leigh, although he had offered to set up the tent for her use. He had also chopped the wood and done the cooking, just as he would have done if he'd been alone.

They had eaten early, freeze-dried stew that Leigh forced down because she needed the calories. By the time the sky began to purple, they were sitting by the fire, finishing the last of the coffee.

Kaler was sitting on a fallen log, watching the fire burning itself to ash. Leigh was sitting on the ground, using the log as a prop for her back. Her eyes were closed, and her breathing was regular. The firelight softened the weariness in her face, but it was still there, just as he'd known it would be.

He'd pushed them both hard, covering the easier ground with few stops. Tomorrow he planned to head due west, toward the heart of Icicle Canyon. He was following a hunch, but under the circumstances, it was all he had.

It would be a rough day, worse than today. Higher altitude. Rougher trail. Leigh would be drawing on reserves before midday.

All this to keep that cold bastard Bradbury alive for another few years, he thought. The man should have died years ago. Maybe then Leigh would stop trying so hard to live up to some imaginary standard of perfection just to please the sainted "ambassador."

Kaler allowed himself a grim smile. He and Bradbury had spent time together exactly twice. Both times they'd circled each other like timber wolves looking for an edge, an advantage to use against the other.

They had disagreed on virtually everything—politics, sports, manners. Every damn thing but one. Both loved Leigh.

He slitted his eyes and searched for the moon. It was just past new, a sliver of silver ice in the sea dark sky. Somewhere in the distance a cougar screamed, then screamed again, the sound carrying easily on the cool night breeze.

Leigh started, and her eyes opened. "I must have dozed off for a minute there. Sorry to be such bad company."

"It's the altitude. Probably take you a day or two get used to it."

"I'm not sure I ever will. I get queasy in elevators."

Her lips formed a self-conscious smile, drawing his attention to the impudent curve of her lower lip. It came swiftly, a powerful need to feel her soft mouth move under his. He'd been celibate too long, he thought grimly.

Leaning forward, he tossed another small piece of wood onto the dying coals. There was a violent hiss of protest, and then the smoldering embers burst into white hot flame, licking voraciously at the fresh fuel.

Leigh downed the last of her coffee. It was more dregs than liquid and left a bitter aftertaste. She dropped the plastic cup into the pan of sudsy water and stretched her aching back.

"Danny was so excited when he left. All he could talk about was sleeping in a tent and cooking over a campfire."

Silence settled around them again, broken only by the seductive whispering of the flames and an occasional rustling far above their heads.

"How old were you when you first went camping?" she asked when the stillness grew unbearable.

"Seventeen. On bivouac during boot camp." Kaler drew a cigar from his pocket and lit it. Smoke curled upward, obscuring his features. The tobacco was the same dark, strong blend he'd always favored, and she remembered the nights they'd lain together in the dark, the glow of his cigar the only light. Shivering, Leigh pulled up her legs and circled her knees with her arms.

From somewhere close she heard the rustle of brush, followed by the scurry of sharp little claws on hard ground. The wind was rising, bringing with it the scent of pine. Overhead, a few lonely clouds were drifting between her and the sickle moon.

Mommy's coming, Danny, she told him silently. Don't be scared.

Fear pushed at her throat, nearly choking her. With all her heart, she wished they were in Danny's impossibly messy room in Phoenix, sipping hot chocolate and playing checkers.

He was such a bright little boy, with a smile that melted even the most cynical heart. My little love, she thought.

Kaler hadn't asked her one question about her son. Nor had he seemed particularly interested when she spoke of Danny. But then, why should he care about a kid he'd never seen? After all, it was more than obvious that he no longer cared about the boy's mother.

She glanced up and caught Kaler's gaze through the fire's glow. "Is this the way it's going to be between us from now on?"

"This?" he asked, before rolling his half-smoked cigar between his strong fingers before studying the glowing tip.

"Yes, this. Or, to be more specific, this silent treatment you've been giving me since we left the ranger station."

"Maybe I've said all I have to say."

"You always were a man of few words, Kaler, but not this few."

Kale took a final puff on his cigar before flipping it into the fire. "I thought I'd buried the past a long time ago. Seeing you again made me realize I hadn't."

"I have a few ghosts to lay to rest myself," she said softly.

Leaning forward, Kaler rested both forearms on his heavy thighs and loosely linked his fingers. He was bareheaded, and the firelight picked up the sun-bleached strands in his thick hair, turning them to bronze.

"I shouldn't have blown up the way I did at Belle's," he said, staring into the fire. "I never did handle surprises very well." He sat back and ran his palms over his thighs. "Next time I show up, she'll likely throw me out for disturbing the peace."

"I doubt that. She's very fond of you."

His quick smile was self-conscious. "She's the closest thing I ever had to a grandmother, only don't let her know I said that. She claims she's only fifteen years older than me."

"She told me about your brother and how he died," she murmured over the soft hissing of the fire. "I'm very sorry, Kaler. I know it must have hurt to lose him that way."

If he was surprised that Belle had talked to her about such private matters, he didn't show it. "He was just a kid from the country. Hell, he'd never even seen the ocean until he got to San Diego."

He got to his feet abruptly and walked toward the edge of the fire's glow, where he stood with his back to her and his hands jammed into his back pockets.

Shutting her out again, she thought sadly, and then felt a moment of surprise when he resumed talking. "I talked him into enlisting, did you know that?"

Leigh shook her head, then realized he wasn't watching her. "No, I didn't."

"I wanted him to have the opportunities I never had— to go to college, to have choices. The marines offered schooling in exchange for a few years' service."

He turned slowly to face her. The firelight played up the stark angles and strong bones of his face, but she could see shadows under his eyes and lines around his mouth. They were deeper now, more from suffering than the added years, she thought intuitively. Kaler had never taken anything lightly, especially his passions. She had a feeling he would feel pain just as deeply.

"I knew guys in Nam smoked dope and took speed and even heroin sometimes when they could get it. It was part of the life over there. But I thought Andy wouldn't have that problem stateside. Dumb, huh?" His eyes crinkled, as though he were going to smile, but his mouth remained hard.

"Andy was the reason you were so determined to get Mendoza and his buddies in the cartel, wasn't he?"

He hesitated, then took the seat he'd abandoned earlier. "It was all I could do. But even when Mendoza sang like a bird and a few of the worst of the pushers ended up doing time, it wasn't enough. It couldn't bring Andy back, or any of the other kids who died or ended up with fried brains."

Leigh suddenly realized that Kaler needed a lot of protecting, from himself, mostly, and the rigid conscience that was driving him harder than she ever could.

"Sometimes...sometimes people do the wrong thing for the best of reasons."

Slowly he turned his head, showing her eyes that were now dark and compelling and still oddly vulnerable. "Some things stay with a man for life. Like the look in your eyes when you found out I wasn't quite the hero on the white horse you thought I was."

She took a deep breath. "I had a lot of naive illusions then. Having Danny has helped me to be more . . . human, I think." She laughed softly. "I hope."

"You were always human to me, Leigh."

"I sure proved it seven years ago, didn't I? I wish—"

Suddenly there was a loud crack, followed by a dull reverberation.

On his feet instantly, Kaler grabbed the gun propped against the log and levered a shell into the chamber. "Stay down," he ordered.

"Can you see anything?"

"Too dark." He was standing perfectly motionless, his head cocked slightly to one side and his gaze efficiently roaming the area.

"Is it a hunter, do you think?"

"More like a poacher," he said in a disgusted growl. "Legal season doesn't start until fall."

"Poaching for what?"

Kaler moved only his eyes, and then for just a split second before they were again trained in the direction of the shot. "Whatever walks on four legs and brings in a few dollars on the black market. Last I heard, bear paws were fetching as much as a hundred each."

Leigh nibbled at her lower lip and tried to see beyond the thick screen of dense pines surrounding them. "Is that why you brought your rifle? Because of the danger of poachers?"

"I always bring it. Habit, I guess." Kaler slowly lowered his rifle, but she noticed that he didn't remove the shell from the chamber.

"Are they gone, do you think?" she asked, already worrying about Daniel and her father. There were accidents all the time in the mountains. Hunters mistaking humans for prey, rock slides, lightning strikes.

"Probably."

Leigh got to her feet and moved closer to the fire. Her back was sore, and her shoulders felt raw where the pack's straps had rested.

"I packed only bright clothes for Danny." She paused to listen to the far-off screeching of an owl. It was an eerie, unsettling sound, far too much like a cry of pain in the night. "Not that I expected anything to happen, but I, well, you know. Just in case."

She heard the rustle of movement and then smelled the rich scent of cigar smoke clinging to Kaler's shirt as he leaned the rifle against the log and joined her in front of the blaze.

"Don't borrow trouble, Leigh. If your father's anywhere close to where he said he'd be, I'll find him."

"It's just that I'm not used to feeling so helpless." There was fear in her eyes and a vulnerable softness in the corners of her sudden frown, although she was doing her best to hide it.

"Hell of a feeling, isn't it? Helplessness."

"I've decided I don't much like it."

"No, you would hate that, wouldn't you?"

It took Leigh a moment to focus her gaze on his face. He was smiling, a canted, off-center smile that took her breath, but his hollowed cheeks were flushed, and his eyes glittered like warm sapphire beneath his drawn eyebrows.

The hard, angry, remote man who'd walked out of Belle's was still there, lurking in his deep-set lonely eyes, but the other man was there, too. The hardheaded, opinionated, lean as a whip and tough as rawhide maverick she'd fallen head over heels in love with sometime during the first hour they'd ever spent together.

"It's late," she managed to murmur past the sudden thickness in her throat. But somehow his fingers had gotten tangled in her hair, and he was nudging her head backward. His gaze dipped to her creamy throat, then lower, to the faint shadow of cleavage hidden below the lapels of her shirt.

Having no place else to go, her hands rested on his chest. Beneath the sweat-stained shirt stretched over hard muscle, his heart rammed violently against his rib cage.

"Maybe not as late as we think."

Don't, she told him, and then realized she'd said the word only in her mind. His hand was gentle as it cupped her chin, and she thought his fingers trembled.

"Just a good-night kiss," he murmured. "For old times' sake."

"I don't think that's a good idea," she whispered, but her mouth was already searching for his.

He seemed to shudder even as his powerful arms drew her closer. He kissed her again and again, each kiss more and more intimate.

Inside, a warm feeling slowly uncoiled from some dark, lonely place until she felt buoyant and eager. Her hands skimmed his unyielding chest, his lumberjack shoulders, his strong sinewy neck. Her fingers pushed eagerly into his thick, sun-warmed hair and rubbed against his scalp.

He made a noise low in his throat, like a predator caught in his own trap, before he lifted his mouth from hers and drew a ragged breath.

"Leigh, honey, we have to stop or I'll end up making love to you in the dirt."

He still had control, he told himself, but he was rapidly losing it. One more sigh, one more soft entreaty, and he would cross that fine line between desire and clawing, punishing hunger.

"I...guess there's more left between us than we thought," she said with a small, shaky smile. "We'll have to be more careful. Agreed?"

Kaler cleared his throat of a sudden thickness. A man could endure hunger and cold and even physical pain far easier than he could endure the kind of loneliness that comes with the end of love.

"Agreed."

Somehow she managed a polite smile before stooping to gather up her toiletry bag. "I'll just use the facilities one more time before I turn in."

Daybreak came early, Kaler thought. He should have been asleep hours ago.

He laced his hands behind his head and stared at the night sky. The North Star shone like a cold, unfriendly beacon. Orion the Hunter brandished his club, alone as always.

He could navigate by those stars and sometimes even predict the weather by the kind of haze obscuring them. He knew animals and their habits and the way their tracks changed when they were spooked or placidly grazing or blind-crazy in rut. He'd learned those things the way he'd learned everything—trial and error. But reading Leigh and her feelings was something else.

Slowly he turned his head and studied the faint glow from the dying fire. No warmth came from the coals, only a lonely wisp of smoke. Not quite an arm's length away, she was curled into her sleeping bag, deeply asleep.

The first few times they'd slept together he'd damn near strangled from all the arms and legs she'd wound around him. Once his subconscious got the message that he wasn't being attacked, he'd come to like having her sleeping on top of him.

His bed at the home place was a single, scarcely bigger than his bunk in the recruit barracks. He barely had room to turn over on the narrow mattress. For a long time, however, it had seemed empty without her sharing it with him.

She had a way of doing that, taking over a man's mind. Hell, she'd once taken over his damn soul. Right from the beginning she'd had him off guard, never knowing what to expect from her next.

Damn near made a fetish out of self-sufficiency and pulling her own weight in a predominantly male world, when he'd expected her to use her femininity to get a cushy desk job. Not her, no way. She'd wanted to do the hard, dirty jobs. The dangerous jobs.

On the obstacle course she'd been a pint-sized, dainty commando in pink sneakers and braids, and so darn determined to finish number one that she'd put in every spare hour practicing. She'd been a crack shot, too, almost as good as Kaler himself. And she'd been the best interrogator he'd ever seen.

Bad guys just naturally trusted her with their deepest darkest secrets—after she'd teased and bullied and charmed them into letting down their guard.

No one would ever have cause to regret partnering Leigh Bradbury, she'd told him on that first day in his office, and no one ever had. Half the senior men in his division had volunteered to work with her by the time he'd gotten around to realizing that he was smitten.

Every time he was around her, his pulse took off like a Fourth of July skyrocket and he started thinking about tangled sheets and skin as soft and milky as a gardenia he'd once seen in a florist's window.

And when he'd touched her for the first time, his body had heated like it had in Nam when he'd been sweating out fever. Lord, her skin had been soft, as soft as that pure white flower had looked to a kid from the sticks.

He'd gone sky-high, higher than any skyrocket, high on the kind of emotional rush that hit most guys around puberty.

There had been a fair number of women who had satisfied his physical needs over the years. Two or three had even drawn him into long-term affairs, and there had been a schoolteacher in San Diego who'd damn near worn him to a nub in bed. But none had ever made him feel as young and innocent as a boy struggling with the awe and wonder of his first love the way Leigh had.

Tenderness, longing, a boy's craving to please—she'd drawn them all from him during the slow, off-again, on-again progression of his courtship.

Courtship, hell, he thought, turning onto his side. He'd been so hot for her that he'd damn near spent more hours under a cold shower than he'd spent working. When they'd finally made love, he'd been as high as an addict on jungle-strength speed for days afterward. God, she'd been sweet.

Though technically not a virgin at twenty-six, she had been awkward and unschooled sexually. He still remembered the awe and humility he'd felt when he'd brought her to her first shuddering climax.

She'd cried from the wonder and happiness of it. He'd damn near joined her, he recalled with a sharp feeling of loss. Nothing had touched him with quite as much intensity as the soft, shimmering look of awe in her brown eyes. Sometimes he thought he must have fallen in love with her at that moment.

No matter what he was doing or wasn't doing, he would find himself remembering the quick surge of expectation he'd felt just before he opened the door and walked into a room where she was waiting. With Leigh, in spite of her education and sophistication, he never felt that he had to guard his words or worry about his grammar or try to figure out how he was measuring up to someone else's standards.

From someplace near, an owl gave a low hoot. Brush rustled as small feet scurried for cover. Powerful wings fluttered overhead as the night hunter made his move. There was a muffled squeal as the marauding predator's claws ripped into the helpless prey. And then silence.

He felt the slick nylon under his back and the heat of the fire on his face. For the past two weeks he'd been listening to a bunch of guys bragging about their kids. The way they told it, their kids were the brightest, the best looking and absolutely destined for the Olympics someday.

Sure, he'd felt a pang of envy. A guy was supposed to want kids, wasn't he? Natural law and all that. Hell, wasn't that the real reason men and women went nuts over each other? A few moments of pleasure, a receptive egg, a few million aggressive little swimmers, and suddenly two people had themselves a baby.

Natural law didn't give a damn if the people were suited to each other or even knew each other. And it sure didn't require them to love each other. Hell, it didn't even require them to care for the kid once it was born. He'd learned that before he'd been out of diapers more than a few short years.

Kaler slowly let his lungs fill with wood-scented air and just as slowly let it out again. He didn't want to think about a little blue eyed kid named Daniel. He didn't want to think about that little boy's mama or how much he wanted the things she'd told him about that little boy to be true.

It was another hour before he finally fell asleep. When he did, he dreamed of a house with a picket fence and a rope swing in the backyard. A house that remained empty, no matter how many rooms he searched through.

Four

Everywhere Leigh looked, she saw beauty and peace, and the air was deliciously clear. The faint breeze rustling through the treetops smelled of pine and cedar and was filled with the sound of bird song.

Beneath the thick branches, pockets of deep shade beckoned, tempting her to kick off her hot, heavy hiking boots and wiggle her toes in the grass.

It was nearly noon. They had been on the trail since first light, with only a couple of brief stops for rest and water. So far she had managed to keep up. Now, however, the altitude and exertion were beginning to tell on her.

Pushing back the brim of her baseball cap, she side-stepped a low-hanging branch, then darted another look at Kaler's back. They would stop soon, she told herself. If he didn't call a halt, *she* would. Even a packhorse needed a breather now and then, she told herself as she glumly regarded the vast expanse ahead.

Chumstick Mountain thrust its jagged peak into the clear blue of the sky. A rare and increasingly precious old growth forest of pines and firs rose majestically to her right. On her left, the ground fell away to fold into a long scythe-shaped canyon that sliced a chunk out of the Chumstick foothills.

According to Kaler, Icicle Creek emptied into a lake at the far end of that canyon. Twenty-five miles as the crow flew—several days walk when she needed it to be hours. Days when Daniel might be alone and vulnerable and wondering why his mommy didn't come for him. Days when—

What was that? she thought, straining for a clearer look. There it was again, a flash of red against the green. Her heart raced. Daniel had been wearing a red shirt when he'd driven away with her father.

Leigh whipped off her sunglasses and stared at the red splotch. It was moving, growing larger. A person, definitely, and not a large one. But, she realized with sinking spirits, definitely larger than a six-year-old.

As the hiker neared, she saw that he was in his late teens or early twenties, and short, no taller than her own five-foot-four-inch frame.

The black lettering on his scarlet T-shirt proclaimed him to be the property of the University of Washington. No doubt a college student enjoying the last days of summer vacation.

"Morning," Kaler said when the stranger came to a stop a few feet away. His rifle remained slung over his shoulder, but Leigh noticed that one hand curled loosely around the strap, just in case he needed it in a hurry. Some habits were hard to break, she thought, or perhaps he hadn't tried to break that one.

The young man pushed back his floppy white hat to reveal bright blue eyes and a sunburned face. He smelled of sweat and bug repellant. "Morning. Great day for a walk, isn't it?"

Kaler nodded, then introduced himself and Leigh. "Been out long?"

"Ten days. Name's Eric Borden, from Olympia. You two just heading out?"

"Second day. We're looking for an older man and a six-year-old boy. Supposed to be heading for Icicle. Seen anyone like that?"

Borden took off his hat and wiped his brow. "Not so's I remember."

Leigh fought to hide her disappointment. "The little boy's about so high—" she held her hand at thigh level "—and he's probably wearing a Phoenix Cardinals cap."

"Sorry. I'll keep my eyes open, though."

"Please, and if you see them, tell my father to go directly to the ranger station and talk to a ranger named Rusty Friedrickson. My father's name is Bradbury. Winston Bradbury."

"Rusty Friedrickson. Winston Bradbury. Got it."

Kaler saluted that with a brief grin. "Where were you camping last?" he asked.

"Near Eagel Creek Spur."

"See any other campfires?"

"I saw some smoke about two, no, three days back. It was due west of Deadman's Rapids." He turned one-hundred and eighty degrees and pointed. "I noticed because the smoke seemed to be coming in . . . in puffs." He turned back and grinned self-consciously. "Like Indian smoke signals, you know?"

Leigh's gaze swung eagerly to Kaler. "Last summer Danny was going through an Indian phase," she said so rapidly that her words tripped over each other. "Father promised to teach him some smoke signals."

Kaler hid his surprise as he turned to thank the kid.

"Hey, no problem," Borden replied with another Huck Finn grin. "Us mountain types have to stick together, you know."

Leigh gave him a warm smile. "Good luck on the rest of your stay." She extended her hand. Borden wiped his own across his belly before returning the handshake.

Kaler watched the kid's Adam's apple bob nervously and remembered his first exposure to Leigh Bradbury. There was something about the warm curve of her smile and the intimate glow in her deep brown eyes that coaxed a guy to believe he was special. Talk to me, her smile urged. Tell me all the things that only you know.

Leigh had to give her hand a gentle tug before the young man remembered to release his grip.

"Uh, nice to meet you, ma'am. You, too, sir. Good luck, okay?" He moved past them and headed down the trail they'd just traveled.

"Oh, Kaler! I feel so much better!" Leigh exclaimed, tilting back her head to meet his gaze. "Smoke signals. It's got to be them. I know it is!"

Hope sparkled like diamonds in her eyes, tugging at him hard. When Leigh allowed herself to show vulnerability, she was damn near irresistible, especially to a man who had spent most of his life taking care of the people he loved.

"Seems like it's only useful if one of us reads smoke signals." He caught a whiff of French perfume and scowled. "I don't, so that leaves you."

"For Pete's sake, it's not important what the darn smoke puffs *said,*" she said impatiently. "What's important is that Father and Daniel were alive three days ago."

One of them, anyway, he thought as he started walking again.

Kaler didn't believe in brooding. It was a waste of time and energy. If a man had trouble eating at his belly, he hunkered down and did something about it—which was why he was wearing himself out chopping more wood than their fire could possibly consume in one night.

A few yards away from the grassy clearing, a fair-to-middling-sized stream rippled under a fallen log forming a natural bridge. The lengthening rays of the sun reached through the branches to dapple the clear water with gold. Clusters of soapsuds floated lazily downstream, reminding him of lacy lily pads. Leigh was taking a bath upstream.

The word he spat out was crude and to the point. It didn't help. Ignoring his burning muscles, he repeatedly sank the razored edge of his hatchet into a length of pine until it split neatly.

The scent of freshly hewn pine and the release of strenuous exercise usually soothed his blackest mood. This evening, however, it only seemed to mock him. It had taken him all of a few hours alone with her on the trail to realize he still wanted her.

Some dumb fools never learn, he thought, as he up-ended another section of pine and steadied it with his foot. He brought the hatchet down hard, splitting the wood cleanly.

"I'm glad it wasn't my head under there."

Kaler whipped his gaze sideways. It had been a long time since anyone had managed to slip up on him unnoticed.

Her face was soft with that just scrubbed look, and her hair hung in damp waves to her shoulders. The oversized white T-shirt that covered her from neck to a scant inch above her short shorts was soaked where the ends of her hair rested a few inches above the soft swell of her breasts.

His mind veered toward an image of soft white skin covered with slippery soapsuds, and a feeling like a groan rippled through his suddenly tense body.

"Have a nice soak?"

"Hmm, lovely. I didn't even mind the minnows that kept nibbling at my toes."

The image in his mind grew dangerously erotic. Once he had been the one nibbling. Her earlobes, her breasts, the downy softness between her legs. With a violent movement of his arm, he sank the hatchet's steel blade into the nearest chunk of wood.

"My turn," he said as he grabbed his towel and the pocket-size waterproof bag holding his razor and a few other toilet articles.

Leigh watched him stride toward her, his face set in unreadable lines, his eyes walled off and distant. While she'd been bathing, he'd removed his shirt, something he apparently did with frequent regularity because his chest and arms were teak dark.

"Coffee's ready," he said as he moved past her. She had watched him working for a moment before speaking and still remembered the ripple of sinuous tendons and sweat-shiny muscles. His body was as beautiful to behold as it had been to love. A feeling very like grief moved through her.

"Watch out for the minnows," she called after him. He disappeared into the trees without responding.

Leigh shifted position. The log she was using as a bench was rough against her bare thighs. Kaler was stretched out on the grass a few feet away, letting his dinner settle before he took a last stroll around before turning in.

Behind them, the tent flap was tied open, letting the evening breeze air out the small space. Inside, their bedrolls lay side by side.

Last night they'd slept under the stars. Tonight, as soon as the sun had dropped behind the western peaks, the temperature had dipped a good ten degrees and showed signs of dipping lower, making shelter advisable. An extremely small shelter.

"How far do you think Father and Daniel have traveled from the spot where that college student saw the smoke signals?"

Kaler rolled onto his side and braced his head on his hand. His shoulders were sore. Not from the physical labor he'd done. Nor from the weight of his pack. From the tension that being with Leigh again had put in him.

"Hard to tell. Traveling with a kid is bound to slow him down. So will the terrain."

"He's not trying to make time."

"How do you know?"

"Because he's looking for something." Leigh dropped her gaze to the half-peeled twig in her hand. Using one perfectly sculpted nail, she picked at the edge of the bark.

Kaler recognized the signs. Leigh could never sit still when she was feeling off balance and insecure. Sometimes she paced. When she couldn't do that, she fiddled—with her hair, the cuff of a blouse, papers on her desk, whatever was handy.

When *he* wasn't as confident as he wanted to be, he hid it behind a black scowl that kept the world at a safe distance.

"What *exactly* is your father looking for?" he asked when he realized she didn't intend to volunteer any more information.

"Oh, tracks, signs of habitation, that sort of thing." The light wasn't completely gone. Enough remained so that Kaler could see embarrassment crossing her face.

"You know it's not hunting season?"

"He's not exactly hunting."

"What *exactly* is he doing, then?"

Leigh stripped another curl of bark from the twig and watched it fall to the grass beneath her bare feet. "He's, um, looking for Sasquatch."

Kaler blinked. "Sasquatch?"

"Yes, Sasquatch," she repeated crossly.

Kaler found himself staring. *This* wasn't even on the list of the things he had been considering as a possible reason for her obvious uneasiness.

When the silence lengthened, Leigh's head came up and her chin tilted. A rebellious look came into her eyes, making them snap.

"Surely you've heard of Bigfoot," she elaborated with exaggerated patience that made her lips curve enticingly. "Yeti? Half man, half human. Shaggy hair, huge feet?"

Kaler found that he had to work to suppress a grin. "I *know* what you mean. I'm just trying to imagine your father, the *ambassador,* trekking through the woods looking for some publicity-hungry idiot's idea of a joke."

Leigh picked another piece of bark free and peeled it away from the slippery wood. "Ever since he's retired, he's had these . . . enthusiasms."

"Eccentricities, you mean."

"No, I mean enthusiasms. Besides, who are you to say that Sasquatch doesn't exist?"

Her mouth turned stubborn, drawing his undivided attention. She had a lovely mouth, soft in the corners, full on the bottom, alluringly sensitive on the top. Easy to kiss all over.

"I'll believe in Bigfoot when I see one."

"Cynic."

"Through and through."

Leigh tossed the now stripped-bare twig into the fire and watched it sputter. Far above, the birds were settling for the night. Their cries were oddly mournful, as though they knew something she didn't.

Fear ran through her like a shiver. She tried to shake it off by reminding herself that she had never been superstitious and wasn't about to start now.

"Don't worry. They're just mountain jays," Kaler said as he stood and stretched out the kinks before hunkering down to build up the fire. The flames leapt wildly, throwing harsh shadows onto his face. The evening breeze had ruffled his hair before it had dried, giving it a boyish unruliness.

Looks were deceptive, she reminded herself. Kaler was capable of cruelty and violence and the deepest bitterness, especially when someone crossed him. Or, worse, hurt him.

Don't hate me, she thought. I did what I had to do. But the guilt that had been simmering inside her since she'd told him about their son suddenly flared as hot as those flames.

Kaler drew a cigar from his pocket and lit it with a brand from the fire. Then he walked into the darkness outside the circle of firelight and stood smoking in silence, savoring the expensive tobacco. Good cigars and fine leather. The preferences of a gentleman.

Kaler had always insisted on both, Leigh realized suddenly. Not because he'd been bred that way, but because that was what he'd instinctively liked. It was that way with most things in his life.

He'd learned to manage subordinates the hard way—in the rice paddies of Vietnam—while she had been learning drawing-room manners at the most prestigious finishing school in Georgetown.

While she'd been in graduate school, studying international law and the latest methods in territorial protection, he'd been risking his life working undercover on loan to the DEA to infiltrate a drug-smuggling ring in Southern California.

Leigh closed her eyes and lifted her face to the wispy breeze. Lord, she had been green. "Report to District Supervisor M. Kaler in Phoenix," her orders had read.

Didn't the man have a first name? had been her first question. Why in the world such a tough-looking, bad-tempered man had been made a supervisor was her second—asked of herself and the Fates a few moments after she'd walked into his neat-as-a-pin office that first morning.

He hadn't stood the way men invariably did when she walked in. Bad manners and eyes hard enough to get the attention of the toughest lawbreaker, she catalogued silently. Impressive bearlike shoulders on a whipcord-lean frame. Thick blond hair that badly needed the attention of a skilled stylist. A lived-in face that had no doubt been devilishly handsome when he'd been younger and less cynical.

"Henrietta Elisabeth Leigh Bradbury?" he'd growled impatiently. "What kind of fancy-pants name is that?"

"Mine," she'd shot back with her most diplomatic, and some said intimidating, smile. It bounced off him without making a dent.

"Former Ambassador Winston Robert E. Lee Bradbury's your father?"

"Yes." She resisted the urge to fidget under the intense scrutiny from those surprisingly intelligent eyes. Ladies were serene under even the most trying circumstances.

"Any relation to the general?"

"Very distant," she murmured with all the modesty her mother had drummed into her.

"Figures," he snorted as he rubbed one big hand across his lean belly, as though talking to her had given him a pain.

"Damn suits in Washington. Last thing I need is a baby-faced debutante to baby-sit," he'd growled at her as he'd scanned the salient facts listed in her transfer papers.

At twenty-six she'd hardly qualified as a debutante and told him so. Respectfully, of course, but with enough fire to make her point.

Having already labeled him a chauvinist like too many of his colleagues, she waited for District Supervisor M. Kaler to explode. Or, worse, to make the kind of crude, sexist remark she'd come to abhor.

Instead he slowly lifted his sharp gaze to hers. His eyes were deep set and a vivid blue, a real contrast to his permanent tan. And years of squinting into the hot desert sun had fanned deep lines at the corners.

Sun-bronzed lashes as thick as a boy's gave him a lazy look, which instinct told her was deceptive—especially when he had fired one question after another at her. About her training, her philosophy, her ambitions. None of the questions were easy, especially the ones posing hypothetical crises.

What would you do if the little old lady with the helpless, fluttery air turned out to be carrying a kilo of heroin stitched into the lining of her shabby bag?

"Arrest her, using established procedures, and then make sure there was a paramedic standing by in case the sweet, little old cork had a heart attack."

What would you do if the baby-faced teenager with Bambi eyes suddenly pulled out a nine millimeter and pointed it at you?

"Shoot to disarm him and hope the sharp-shooting medals I won weren't flukes."

What would you do if some hard-ass chauvinist made a pass at you in his office?

"Deck him."

His grin, surprisingly and endearingly boyish, caught her by surprise. By its suddenness, first of all, and then by the soft shivers of purely feminine response that ran through her. Perhaps he wasn't quite as unattractive as she'd first thought.

"You'll do," he said in a low rumbling voice that she soon discovered could grow as soft as a sigh when he whispered words of need against her mouth.

As she'd shaken the big hand he'd offered, she'd felt her insides bunch into a strangely pleasurable tension. Without even knowing how, she'd been caught, trembling inside like a newly emerged butterfly....

"We're going to get a rain tonight." His voice came out of the thick darkness to her left, recalling her to the present.

"Kaler," she whispered with a nervous laugh. "I'd forgotten what a soft-walking man you can be when the mood strikes you."

He came into the light, seeming larger than life silhouetted against the now star-bright sky. She expected him to return to the soft cushion of the grass. Instead he came to sit next to her on the log. The mingled scents of smoke and soap clung to his skin, and the red tip of his cigar glowed in the gathering darkness.

The logs burned steadily, lulling her into a half doze. A dull soreness had settled in her calves and shoulders, impervious so far to the three aspirin she had swallowed after dinner.

She stifled a yawn behind her hand and, looking up, tried to focus her tired eyes on the Milky Way, but suddenly it seemed to blur in and out of focus.

Hang on, Danny, she thought. Mommy's coming.

She could see his eyebrows bunching in a scowl at the very idea. He was already such a toughie. So masculine, even when he was a toddler driving her crazy with his energy and curiosity. So like the little boy she had imagined Kaler to have been.

Closing her eyes, she pictured Danny and Kaler together—one so large and strong and obstinately proud, the other filled with the same promise of strength and stubborn pride.

"Leigh?"

"Hmm?" It had been a long time since she'd been alone with a man in the moonlight. Even longer since she'd wanted to nestle into his arms and raise her face for his kiss.

"Tell me about the boy."

Suddenly uncomfortable, she forced a bright smile. "He's the brightest, cutest, sweetest kid in the world."

His mouth quirked. "Why did you name him Daniel?"

"Actually, it's Winston Daniel. I named him for my father and...and Edward's."

Beyond the light of the campfire where she was sitting, it was getting very dark. Leigh realized that she was glad.

"And his last name?"

"Pinchot."

His lashes flickered, the only sign of reaction he allowed himself. "Sounds French."

"It is."

Kaler felt his muscles stiffening and sat up. "Old money, of course."

"Yes. His father and mine are good friends. Edward and I had known each other since kindergarten."

"Old money and Southern aristocracy. Sounds like a perfect match." Sometimes, especially after they'd made love, Kaler's deep blue eyes had taken on a searching look, as though he were seeking something more from her. Something important. They were doing that now.

"Everyone said so."

"Did he know that you were carrying another man's child when he married you?"

The heat that surged into her face had nothing to do with the fire. "He knew everything about me. And you."

Heartbroken and disillusioned after Kaler's resignation, she had taken some long overdue vacation time and gone home to lick her wounds. There she found her childhood beau waiting to court her again. He loved her, he said. But there was this little problem with his heart.

Congenital weakness, the doctors had said. Damn Virginia inbreeding, Edward had laughingly maintained. Five years max, they'd given him. When he'd admitted that he wanted to spend those years with her, to give his name to a child that would live on after him, Leigh couldn't refuse. They'd been happy for three precious years, and then, suddenly, Edward was gone.

Leigh closed her eyes and arched her neck, trying to relieve the tightness that had grown steadily worse. "In a strange way, I think you and Edward could have become good friends."

"How did he die?"

"Heart attack, during bypass surgery. He knew the odds were against him, but he took the chance because..." Her voice trailed off.

"Because?" Kaler prompted.

"Because he thought Daniel deserved a father who could take him skiing and teach him to throw a forward pass."

Kaler stared into the fire and realized that he couldn't do either one. Daniel had been lucky to have a man like Edward for as long as he had.

"He must have been a hell of a guy."

"He was. I miss him a lot."

"Did you love him?"

"Yes, I loved him. Not the way I loved you, but we understood each other." She rose and squared her shoulders. "But, as you told me when you walked out on me, nothing lasts forever."

Five

Kaler squatted on his haunches. His thigh muscles bunched beneath the khaki twill, and his calves bulged from the strain. He looked uncomfortable, but Leigh knew he could sit that way for hours if he had to. If his heavy muscles cramped, he would make no sign. If he grew tired, no one would know.

"What is it?" Leigh leaned closer, her gaze directed at the ground. They were near a sparsely wooded area where a separate section of the hiking trail looped toward the creek a dozen yards farther south. The marks, more like scratches in the dirt, were so faint that Leigh would have walked right past them if Kaler hadn't stopped her.

"Footprints. Two sets. A man and a child. Both wearing hiking boots."

"Father and Danny!"

Leigh bent closer still for a better look. Her breasts hovered just above his shoulder, and her skin exuded the familiar scent of mountain violets.

Only Leigh would wear perfume in the woods, Kaler thought irritably. The delicate scent had tormented him through a restless night trapped in the tent only a few feet away from her. It still tormented him.

"Don't get excited. These tracks are at least two days old."

"How do you know that?"

"See how dry the ground is? And the cracks? I figure two mornings' worth of dew softened the dirt, made it swell, and then the sun made it shrink again."

Leigh was fascinated with the skillful way his fingers feathered over the shallow indentation in the pebbly dirt, lingering here and there almost lovingly. He had sensitive hands, crisscrossed with prominent veins and ridged with callused muscle. His fingers were long, the tips blunt. Leigh had never quite forgotten the feel of those hands on her body.

She straightened, spilling her shadow over the tracks Kaler was still studying. "But you can follow them, right? I mean, it should be easy."

"Nothing's easy in the wild, Leigh." Abruptly he stood and brushed the trail dust from his hands.

"But—"

Kaler cut her off. "Listen!"

Leigh looked around quickly. "What...a dog? Here?" Barking furiously, too, as it raced down a wooded incline fifty yards or so to their left.

Kaler recognized the huge animal instantly. It was a mixed-breed hound, with a coat of short buff-colored bristly hair and a liver-brown muzzle, bred for strength and savagery and trained to kill.

"Get behind me," Kaler ordered, levering a shell into the carbine.

"What?"

"Damn it, Leigh! Get behind me now or you might just lose one of those sexy legs of yours."

"But... my God, you mean it intends to attack us?"

"There's no intending to it."

Leigh spied a dead branch about the size of a baseball bat half buried in the thick carpet of pine needles, and she hurried to fetch it. It felt solid in her hands and, though a bit too long to handle with ease, would serve as a makeshift club.

"Get back here!" Kaler shouted as he raised the rifle to his eye and took a bead on the dog's head. She obeyed, but only after she had the branch firmly in hand.

Kaler closed one eye, lined up the sights and waited. The old carbine had a short range, and its low-caliber bullet needed to be sent true in order to kill anything larger than a deer.

"Wait!" Leigh called urgently. "There's a man up there, trying to get your attention." From what she could see, he was dressed in camouflage and carried a rifle in the crook of his arm.

Leigh heard Kaler mutter a curse and noticed that his finger tensed around the trigger. "Call him off, Guntar, or he's dead!" he shouted. *"Now!"*

"Hold, Bullet!" The bellow halted the dog in his tracks, a few ounces of trigger-pull away from death. Teeth still bared to attack, the animal panted hard, saliva dripping from his mouth. Kaler didn't relax, even though he lowered the rifle a few inches.

"Do you know that man?" Leigh asked as she swept off her hat and wiped her face with the bandanna she impulsively plucked from his back pocket.

"I know him. His people had the place next to ours. Max and I grew up together."

"Max?"

"Maximillian. We have the same first name."

Leigh noticed that his index finger was still curled loosely around the trigger and that his legs were braced in his favorite firing position. She stole another quick look at the running man, before returning her gaze to Kaler's stony profile.

"You don't sound too happy to see him."

"I'm not. Someone should have shot him years back, when there wasn't much in the way of law around here."

"Do you think he's the one who fired the shot we heard the other day?" she persisted.

"I wouldn't bet against it. Word is Max Guntar will do anything for money, legal or not. Trouble is, no one's been able to prove it, not even the law. One man who tried, Belle's son Ron, ended up dead in a ditch. Case is still open. No clues, not even a slug in the body. Whoever did it used exploding bullets. All that was left were a few fragments of lead."

Leigh gasped. "But surely—"

"Thought that was you hollering at me, Kale, old buddy!" the man called when he was within twenty yards.

Leigh drew a sharp breath. It was almost as though she were seeing another version of Kaler—a bloated, dissipated mirror image.

The two men stood head to head in height and appeared to be approximately the same weight, although Kaler carried his bulk in his shoulders and chest, while Guntar's had slid to the beer gut pushing at the buttons of his army surplus fatigues.

"Near to had me a heart attack when I seen you sightin' in on ol' Bullet there," Guntar said with a smirk when he was close enough for Leigh to see his eyes. Bloodshot and calculating, they were the same brilliant blue as Kaler's and framed by the same thick sun-bleached lashes. The stubborn set of the jaw was the same, too, although Guntar's sported at least a two-day growth of whiskers.

At the moment, he was grinning at her through that beard while his bleary gaze slowly looked her up and down. The openly lascivious gleam that came into his eyes when they zeroed in on hers gave her a chill. It also made her revise her opinion of the resemblance between the two men. Maximillian Guntar and Maximillian Kaler were nothing alike.

"How do, pretty lady," he said in a rough whiskey tenor. "My name's Max, and I sure would like to know yours."

"Not while your dog is eyeing me like a filet mignon," she muttered.

Guntar's fleshy lips parted in a grin, revealing stained front teeth, one of which was rimmed with gold. "You must be the gal everyone's talkin' about. The one who sent ol' Kale here slammin' outta the Orchard the other morning."

Kaler moved slightly so that his shoulder was wedged between Guntar's body and Leigh's. "You got a permit to bring a rifle onto state land?"

Guntar feigned surprise. "Permit? What you talkin' about, Kale? You an me used to hunt this land all the time in the good ol' days, or have you forgot?"

"That doesn't mean it was legal."

"Wasn't legal to sell them deer hides we got, neither, but we did."

The dog yipped suddenly, and Leigh realized that the creature had gradually crept forward until it was less than a long leap away.

"Shut up, dog!" Guntar snapped, his face changing into an ugly snarl. "Or by God I'll ram this here rifle barrel down your throat."

Whining deep in his powerful throat, the dog lowered his muzzle to his paws and fixed eager eyes on his master. Poor thing, Leigh thought before Guntar's voice commanded her attention again.

"Word is, you're lookin' for some of your kin."

Leigh kept her expression noncommittal. Inside, she was feeling more and more uneasy. "My father and my son. Perhaps you've seen an older man with a six-year-old boy?"

"Ain't seen nobody but you two." He slanted Kaler a sly look. "Me'n' Bullet are takin' us a vacation."

"Vacation from what—poaching?"

"Poachin'? What the hell you talkin' about, Kale? I haven't made me an illegal kill since we was shirttail kids fightin' to see who bagged the most meat."

"Pretty heavy artillery for target shooting." Kaler's gaze flicked to the heavy-caliber rifle in Guntar's thick arms. It was a Remington 30-06 equipped with a sophisticated scope. The safety was off.

Guntar glanced down, then grinned as he shifted his gaze from the Remington to Kaler's smaller carbine. "You ought to try it sometime, Kale, instead of that old pea-shooter your daddy palmed off on you."

Leigh sensed a shift in the air, reminding her of the sudden stillness just before a violent storm. There was more between these two men than a long-ago rivalry between boys.

"What's the bounty on cougar hides these days?" Kaler's voice was suddenly cold and hard.

"If I knew, I'd be pretty damn dumb to admit it, wouldn't I?"

Kaler's mouth slanted sardonically. "Max, you aren't even smart enough to be considered dumb. You never were."

Guntar's eyes became slits, and his mouth turned ugly. "Stay out of my business, Kaler. You might'a whipped me once when we was kids, but that don't mean diddly now." His oily gaze slid to Leigh's face before dropping to her breasts. The tension surrounding them turned electric, and Leigh felt her spine stiffening.

"Yes, sirree, Kale, you sure got yourself a lot of woman here. Wouldn't want anythin' to happen to her now, would we?"

Behind him the dog suddenly bared its teeth in a menacing growl, as though responding to some private signal from his master.

"Don't even think about it, Max," Kaler warned in the softest of voices, his gaze steely. Leigh watched uneasily as each man took the measure of the other.

"Is that a threat?" Guntar said finally. He kept his chin up and his gaze steady, but Leigh knew he had just blinked first.

"Think of it as advice from someone who's known you a long time," Kaler told him with a cool half smile. "I'd take it, if I were you."

It was well past midnight when Leigh woke to the sound of rain pelting the small conical tent.

A few inches to her right Kaler was lying motionless, deeply asleep. The cadence of his breathing was even and untroubled, bringing a wistful smile to her lips.

That, at least, hadn't changed. During the day Kaler rarely stopped. Once he closed his eyes, however, he seemed to shut down completely, sleeping as single-mindedly as he did everything else.

Her smile faded. Once they would have been intimately intertwined, his hard leg between hers, his hand cupping her breast, her hand cupped over his chest. After a time, she hadn't been able to rest comfortably unless his face was tucked against her shoulder.

Kaler had been her rock, a man of integrity and honor and strength. It had taken time for the bond to grow between them, but when it had, she'd never once doubted the intensity of his love. Or her own. Her trust in him had been complete. Until he himself had shattered it.

Staring into the blackness, she tried to forget the harsh words she had hurled at him. Accusing words. Words to strip away his dignity. Words intended to hurt him as painfully as he'd hurt her. Words about truth and integrity and honor. He had broken the rules, and she had condemned him for it.

Leigh squeezed her eyes shut and bit down hard on her lower lip. Guilt was a new emotion for her, one she'd rarely felt before. Her father had raised her to be scrupulously honest, to maintain the highest standards, to strive for perfection.

She was perfect, all right, she thought with a wince. No mistakes for her. No weaknesses. No flaws. Not Leigh Bradbury. She would never do the things Kaler had done, no matter what the provocation.

The lightning came suddenly, so bright it blinded her. Heart pounding, she sat up quickly, hugging herself against the sudden chill as the moist, cool air hit skin toast-warm from her sleeping bag.

"Kaler?" she said anxiously into the smothering blackness. "Are you awake?"

"I am now." His voice came from someplace low on her left side and still carried the gravelly rasp of sleep.

Lightning cracked again splitting the dark with a brilliant fluorescence. He was lying on his back, with one arm flung over his head and one knee raised. His eyes were half-open and focused in her direction.

"It's raining."

"Could'a fooled me."

Thunder rumbled in the distance, but she couldn't tell if the storm was coming closer or receding. Kaler would know, of course. He'd always been more at home in the outdoors than she was.

She winced as a gust of wind threw the rain against the tough fabric of the tent. Or was that hail she was hearing? She huddled into her sweatshirt and reminded herself that she loved storms.

"Won't the rain cause the creek to flood?" she asked when the silence inside the fragile shelter became oppressive.

"Probably. In the low spots for sure."

Leigh pictured herself ankle-deep in mud and sighed. "Father's tracks!" she cried. "The rain will wipe them out, won't it?"

"Bound to."

Leigh thought she detected a note of masculine amusement in his tone and she stiffened. "Aren't you *worried?*"

She heard the faint rustle as he moved. When he spoke again, his voice was disturbingly close. "No reason. Sounds like you're doing enough for both of us."

Leigh opened her mouth, then shut it. He was right, she thought as lightning flashed again, lighting up the cramped space. The thunder came swiftly this time.

"The storm's coming closer," she muttered.

"Scared?"

"No, worried. Father packed a tent, but not a row-boat."

"I hate to tell you this, Leigh, but neither did we."

Kaler had intended her to laugh, and she did. He hadn't intended to feel a warm rush of desire as the sound rolled toward him in the dark like a caress.

He switched on the propane lamp. Because Leigh wasn't expecting it, she was blinded for a split second.

"What's wrong?" she cried, blinking furiously, her eyes searching for his. Her dark hair was tousled, and her mouth was pale. Her long lashes made provocative little shadows on her clear skin.

"I know how you hate to admit it when you're upset. I wanted to check."

"I'm not afraid of storms."

Tension banded across Kaler's shoulders. He liked her best when she was still sleep-warm and soft-eyed. Her first smile of the day had invariably been drowsy and so damn kissable. A man could stomach a lot of grief, just knowing he had a woman like that waiting for him in his bed. Or hers.

"Remember the night when we made love in front of the fire during the worst cloudburst of the decade?" He took her hand and balanced it on his palm. When she tried to pull away, he closed his fingers, trapping her.

"I remembered that your roof leaked."

"On me, not you. And you licked the raindrops off my chest with your tongue." He brought her hand to his mouth and touched the tip of his tongue on the spot on her wrist where the pulse was strongest.

Her breath caught, drawing his gaze to her lips. He smiled in an endearing, lopsided way that made her brace herself.

"It was good, wasn't it? You and me together?" he asked, leaning forward until she was close enough to see the slightly darker circles rimming his deep blue irises.

"That was then."

"And now?" His head dipped lower until his mouth hovered over hers.

"Now we're just two people who used to know each other," she whispered.

"Two people who share something special."

"Something special?"

"A child, remember?"

Her breathing stopped, but her pulse leapt. She tried to answer him, to be as calm and matter-of-fact as he was being, but her voice seemed to have deserted her.

"Are you afraid of me, Leigh?" With his free hand, he played with a lock of hair that had curled close to her ear. Soft as gosling down, he thought, winding it slowly around his finger.

"Should I be?"

"Absolutely!"

She had forgotten how irresistible Kaler's grin could be when he let himself relax. He tucked her hand against his shoulder, freeing his hand so he could flatten it against her cheek. His palm was cool to her heated skin.

"Tell me about my son, Leigh. Does he look like me?"

The glint in his eyes frightened her into swallowing hard. "He's fair, like you, with blue eyes, but most people say he looks a lot like me."

Does he have your smile? he wondered. Does his have that same mischievous slant when he's pleased with himself?

"Why didn't you tell me you were pregnant?"

"You were gone." Leigh wouldn't allow herself to show weakness by shifting away from him.

"You knew where I'd gone. It was never a secret."

Thunder cracked again, startling her. "What would you have done if I had told you?" It was a coward's ploy, she knew, to throw the spotlight back on him, but he had backed her into a very uncomfortable corner.

Kaler used his fingers to mess up her hair because he liked it better wild, then smiled as the springy curls twined around his fingers.

"I take care of my own, Leigh. That includes any children I might have unknowingly fathered. But then, I suspect you knew that."

Her answer was in the momentary softening of her expression. Her mask of indifference had a few weak spots, he thought with grim satisfaction. So did his, but he'd had more practice at hiding his deepest feelings. Some feelings, however, he didn't have to hide, like his need to kiss her again.

He slid his hand to her throat and used his thumb to lift her chin. She would have moved then, but his fingers curved around her neck with just enough pressure to prevent her escape. He wanted to feel the silk of her mouth against his.

Leigh opened her lips to protest, but his mouth was suddenly warm on hers. He tasted of coffee and a strong man's unspoken loneliness.

"Remember how good it feels to make love in a storm?" he whispered between kisses.

"No," she murmured, but his tongue swirled against her mouth, tempting her. Tantalizing her.

Lightning and thunder came again, this time nearly simultaneously. The feeling that passed through Leigh was primitive, a blending of ancient terror and elemental fascination.

Her mouth trembled, then yielded. She arched her neck and found her arms twining around his neck. She wanted to feel more, skin against skin, hair-roughened masculine legs sliding against hers, hard warm flesh slipping into her until she was filled and complete again.

When he lifted his head and pulled away, she whimpered a low, soft protest. Yes, baby, yes, he thought as he bathed her face in soft seductive kisses, concentrating on her cheeks first and then the small cleft in her chin and the tip of her nose—everywhere but her mouth. Moaning, she turned her mouth toward his, desperate to feel the pliant warmth of his lips pressing against hers.

"It's still there, the fire," he murmured, his eyes glittering with a strange light. She moaned again, framing his face with eager hands to pull his mouth down to hers. He braced his hands and resisted easily. "Do you want me, Leigh? Do you?"

Leigh gave him a dazed frown. His eyes were dark with an emotion she didn't recognize. His breathing was strained, his face flushed. She curved her mouth into a soft, not-quite-steady smile.

"Yes, I want you," she whispered eagerly, reaching for him. Her mouth was eager and hot. "I need you."

He tasted that need then, a searching, seeking need that had nothing to do with sex. She was reaching out to him, a scared, brave woman who suddenly needed someone to hold her in the dark.

A friend. Not a lover. Not a scarred, bitter man who had locked most of his feelings away for good.

His kisses turned gentle, soothing instead of seducing. "It's all right," he said between gentling kisses. "Everything will be all right."

He wrapped his arms around her and nuzzled her neck until he felt her frantic breathing ease into a calmer rhythm and her body relax.

He kissed her mouth and felt it tremble. With the back of his hand he smoothed the silk of her hair away from her forehead before lightly touching his mouth to the faintly lingering worry lines.

"I don't... this isn't like me," she whispered, close to tears. "I keep thinking about Daniel, thinking he might be alone and scared and waiting for me to come and find him."

He brushed her mouth with his thumb. "No one can be strong all the time. Not even you."

"You are."

Kaler shook his head. "No, Leigh, I'm not."

"You never needed anyone, not even me."

"I needed you. I just didn't know how to admit it."

He'd never quite managed to live up to the image she'd had of the perfect man. Maybe that was what had brought everything crashing down on them. He kissed her again, a gentle kiss of comfort, before rolling away from her.

"Kaler?" she called softly, staying his hand that was reaching toward the lamp. Her lips were slightly parted and still softened from the pressure of his mouth, and her eyes were bruised, making her seem dazed and vulnerable.

"Hmm?" He turned back reluctantly, already regretting the things he'd told her about himself that he shouldn't have.

"Thank you for stopping before things got out of hand. For understanding."

"No problem." In spite of the hot pressure in his groin, he managed a passable imitation of a smile, one that she returned shakily, but her eyes burned with anguish.

"Move over," he ordered gruffly.

"Why?" He read confusion in her eyes now and the last lingering trace of desire, desire that a man who had any skill at all could fan into fire. And then what? he thought. More guilt to add to his already overburdened conscience?

"Because I don't want to sleep alone tonight any more than you do."

"Oh." While she hastened to scoot sideways, he slid his sleeping bag closer to hers and stretched out on top of it before patting the empty space between them. "Just sleep, Leigh. I promise."

"You don't have to make promises to me, Kaler. I trust you. I've always trusted you."

Her eyes were smudges of exhaustion in her face as she nestled next to him. But not enough, he thought as her hair slid like warm water over his bare chest and her scent perfumed the air.

"Better now?" he asked, his lips brushing the top of her head. He'd made his share of mistakes. Some unconsciously, some deliberately, but this had to top them all.

"Mmm. Are you?"

"Sure." He curled his arm around her, holding her close. She felt cuddly and small against his bulk, and so damn fragile, like a butterfly he'd once held in his hand.

Rain pelted the tent in a steady, hypnotic rhythm, and soon he felt her relaxing against him.

Sometime later lightning cracked, more distant now, and she moved restlessly, her thigh sliding against his to rest close to his groin.

Gritting his teeth, Kaler rode out the sudden flare of desire stabbing between his legs until the worst of it eased off.

Through tension-slitted eyes he stared at the rich brown silk of her hair spread like lace over his chest. Her hand was curled around his, her fingers relaxed now in sleep.

Slowly, trying not to disturb her, he reached out and turned off the lamp, plunging the tent into utter darkness again.

Thunder rumbled in the distance, and the rain gentled until it was a pleasant drone on the tent's fabric. It hit him then, a longing so strong and deep that it all but took his breath—years and years of longing. To matter to someone. To be special to one special person. To be needed the way Leigh had needed him tonight. Kaler closed his eyes and listened to the rain. One lapse in judgment, he thought. A stupid concession to an obsession that mattered only to him, and suddenly he'd lost everything.

He stood it as long as he could, but gradually the air in the tent became too thin to breathe and the darkness too thick, suffocatingly thick.

Tension skittered down his thighs, turning them hard and tight. The heat in his groin had cooled to a deep throbbing ache that bordered on unbearable, and his belly felt hollow, as though he were totally empty inside.

Slowly he slid from under her, then gently, working by feel only, cocooned her in the warm downy bags. He crouched awkwardly next to her, listening to the soft whisper of her breathing.

A wife. A child. Some men took such gifts for granted. He knew better. He also knew they were not for him, not when he had little more to offer than a ramshackle place on the edge of a mountain and a lot of regrets.

One swift movement took him to the tent flap. Another had him jerking it open. Barefoot, clothed only in running shorts, his skin burning and his body aching, he thrust himself into the storm.

Six

___

Leigh woke slowly. Even before she forced open her eyelids, she knew she was alone. Kaler's side of the tent had been stripped bare. No sleeping bag, no pack, no lantern. Nothing but the sturdy black weave of the tent's flooring.

The smell of coffee drew her attention toward the open flap. The rain had stopped, and the birds were singing. The sun was already high, the sky a blaze of blue. The trees within her narrow view were fresh-washed a brilliant green.

Hurriedly, knowing she had overslept, she scrambled from her sleeping bag and hooked her towel around her neck before fishing into her pack for clean underwear and her toiletry bag.

The air had an invigorating crispness as she stepped barefoot from the tent and filled her lungs. Like champagne sipped from delicate crystal, she thought as she exhaled.

Kaler was crouched over the campfire, his broad back toward the tent. He was dressed in shorts and a clean white T-shirt, but his hiking boots were already coated with mud from the sodden ground.

She hadn't made a sound, but he looked up anyway, reminding her that he'd always had an almost supernatural sensitivity to his surroundings.

"You're just in time. Your eggs à la Kaler are almost ready." Steam curled from the skillet in the center of the metal grill he'd fitted over the fire. He banged the spatula on the side of the pan before lifting it from the fire to a nearby flat rock.

"Certainly the highlight of my day."

"Watch your mouth, lady. The cook isn't in the best of moods this morning."

His eyes were rimmed with red, his face haggard, as though he'd gotten even less sleep than she had. The look on his face was a mixture of badly concealed hunger and gritty resolution.

Flushing, Leigh glanced at her wrist, then remembered that she'd stuffed her watch into her pack before she'd gone to bed. "What time is it?"

"Just past seven."

An hour later than they'd risen yesterday. "Why didn't you wake me?"

"I knew you would wake up when you were ready."

"I smelled the coffee."

"Figured you would."

Toes curling in the still-wet grass, she padded toward her water bottle near the fire.

"You have five minutes," Kaler said as she turned toward a nearby clump of underbrush.

She stopped and glanced back. "For what?"

Kaler noticed that the smudges were gone from her eyes, but her skin was still too pale, and there was a self-conscious tightness around her mouth. She was probably thinking about last night and what had almost happened.

What should have happened, damn it.

"On second thought, you just ran out of time." He stood up, his movements fluid and determined and far too sexy for a woman to handle before she'd had her coffee.

His arms came around her, and he kissed her without restraint, his mouth hard and aggressive. Heat flared, as hot as surprise, before her mouth seemed to soften of its own accord.

His mouth swept over her cheek to find her ear. "I think I like you best in the morning," he said with wicked solemnity. "With your mouth naked and soft and your hair a mess."

Kaler ran his hands slowly through the sherry-brown waves and watched the ends curl wildly around his fingers. Slowly he lifted a strand to his nose and inhaled.

"Smells good, too." Like wildflowers in full bloom, he thought, and then wondered where that poetic nonsense had came from.

"Yours needs cutting," she murmured, ruffling the shaggy sun-streaked ends. His hair had a way of feathering over his neck when it got too long.

"Are you volunteering?" he asked, his mouth hovering over hers again.

"Hmm?" She shouldn't want his kisses. They were dangerously addictive, like the dark cordial-filled chocolates she kept hidden in her desk drawer.

Kaler watched her eyes darken and grow softly unfocused, the way they always did when she wanted to make love. His own desire sharpened and coalesced into a throbbing, insistent ache.

Bracing himself, he nudged her legs apart with his knee and rubbed his thigh against the soft mound between her legs. "Just thinking about doing this nearly drove me crazy."

Leigh gasped as she leaned into the hard thigh rubbing her seductively. "We don't want this," she murmured.

"Speak for yourself, woman." He wasn't holding her so tightly that she couldn't move away. The problem seemed to be in her, she realized as she touched her tongue to his.

His groan shook them both. He pried open her mouth with the moist warm tip of his tongue, then wet her lower lip thoroughly, seductively, before letting his tongue dart and retreat in a slow, tantalizing rhythm.

Leigh needed to get closer, to rub the painful fullness of her nipples against his chest, to feel more of him, but somehow she ended up jabbing him in the belly with the stiff corner of her vinyl toiletry bag.

He drew back, his expression sheepish and his eyes smoldering. "Is that a warning?"

"I think it had better be," she murmured, her lips slightly numb and swollen. "Don't you?"

His little-boy grin came quickly, startling and beguiling her at the same time. "Hell no, but what do I know? I'm just the guide."

After bracing both hands gently on her shoulders, he turned her toward the bushes and gave her a swat on the fanny to get her going.

"Five minutes. And this time I mean it."

The trail angled upward, a cleft in the rocks, narrowing between thick stands of stunted pine and mountain laurel. Wind and erosion had denuded the rock face to the left. Bristle weed grew in the crevices, adding the only hint of color to the bleached granite face.

Footing was precarious in places, forcing Kaler to slow his pace. Now and then he cast a glance over his shoulder to make sure Leigh was still in sight.

She was wearing her baseball cap again—to keep the sun from blinding her, he surmised, since the air was still cool, almost crisp, even though the morning was giving way to midday. Her cheeks were pink, and she licked her lips every few seconds.

Kaler shortened his stride and let her catch up. "There's a pocket meadow over the next rise. We'll stop there."

"Thank God," she muttered, too tired even to smile.

Kaler let her lead the way, this time adjusting his pace to hers. That, he soon discovered, was a mistake. Her shorts, a perfectly modest length, nevertheless managed to cup her bottom provocatively until he found himself hot just watching her walk.

Knowing he was only courting trouble, he let his gaze linger on the lithe length of her thighs. Leigh had the kind of legs a man fantasized about in the shower, when his hands were slippery with soap and his defenses were lulled by the steam. He thought about running his fingers over the soft inner curve where her skin was warmest and her flesh the most tender.

He closed his eyes for a split second and tried to drive the thought from his mind. Sex wasn't the only thing he wanted from her. Probably because it had never been just sex with Leigh, he admitted after a moment's reflection.

It had started with sex, however. As soon as she'd walked into his office and flashed him that classy finishing-school smile, he'd wanted to find out what was behind the polish and style.

He'd found out. Passion, fire and the kind of natural sensuality that couldn't be taught. The debutante from Virginia had been a man's dream. Elegant in public, wanton behind the locked bedroom door. She had given all of herself there, allowing him free access to her thoughts and dreams and emotions.

It had come slowly, the need to love her as strongly as she'd seemed to love him. Even then, he'd fought it. A man was vulnerable when he loved so deeply. It tempted him to drop his guard. To relax. He'd done all those things with Leigh. Once. But never again.

The meadow was in sight when he spied the broken twigs and flattened grass. Someone or something had walked through the underbrush recently. "Leigh, wait!" he called sharply.

Obeying, she turned to give him an eager look. "Do you see something?"

Two strides brought him close enough to see the anxious trembling of her mouth as she searched his face. Swiftly, silently, he shrugged off his pack and rested it against the nearest rock. Still without speaking, he helped her remove hers before taking up his rifle and a box of ammunition.

"Do you think it's Guntar?"

He slipped a handful of .22 caliber bullets into one of the front pockets of his summer-weight hunting vest before acknowledging her with a brief glance. "Possibly."

"Where?"

He nodded toward the meadow. In the sunlight the grass seemed a vivid emerald, and pockets of fading blue lupines and Scotch broom hugged the tree-shaded perimeter.

"Wait here."

He moved forward slowly and as silently as possible, his gaze fixed on the ground ahead. As he walked, he listened. Even though the day was crystal bright and benign, the birds had stopped singing.

Seconds later, in a cul-de-sac formed by towering boulders, he discovered the reason. Bits of matted buff-colored hair and fragments of bone were scattered everywhere. A few yards farther into the shadowed canyon, he discovered the carcass of Guntar's dog. Shredded bits of meat still clung to the crushed ribs.

He scowled and tried not to think of poor Bullet's last few minutes. From the signs, the animal had put up quite a fight. Blood had splattered the granite and pooled into a thick film on the hard dirt.

Crouching, he touched a finger to the black ooze. Underneath, the blood was bright red and obscenely wet where the hardpan prevented it from soaking into the earth. Two or three hours old, he decided grimly as he slowly straightened.

Moving deliberately, he followed the distinctive tracks away from the kill. They led him down a slight rise to a shaded spot where other tracks merged until they were all mixed together.

Shaded most of the day by boulders, the earth was still damp from the rain, making the killer's distinctive tracks clearly visible. The other footprints were clear, too. Two sets, human—one much larger and deep, the other smaller and shallow. A man and a child.

Turning, he scanned the surrounding area. A hundred yards ahead, the trees closed in again, making passage treacherous. Absently he rubbed his thumb over the Winchester's trigger guard.

If he were alone . . .

Even as his senses registered movement and sound, he was folding into a crouching turn, his rifle already aiming. Leigh's face was white and her mouth was open behind the fingers pressed to her lips.

"I saw the blood, the mess." Her voice was flattened, as though she were fighting hard not to scream. "All that's left of Bullet."

His wild heartbeat was still adrenaline fueled. Kaler lowered the rifle and flipped the safety. "Leigh—"

"What kind of creature did that?"

He considered lying, but he respected Leigh too much to treat her as a child to be protected from the big bad world.

"A cougar."

She nodded slowly. "Guntar... you knew he was hunting a cougar. *This* cougar."

"I guessed."

"Did he shoot it? After it killed his dog, I mean?"

He hesitated. "There's no sign that he did. Not here, anyway."

She walked to a large flat rock and sat down slowly. If she just concentrated on breathing all this would go away somehow and she would be back in Phoenix watching Danny playing in the pool with his buddies.

"Your rifle," she said after a few restorative breaths. "The one that seems to be a permanent part of your shoulder. It's not just a habit, is it?"

"No."

"In fact, if I were forced to guess, I'd say that you rarely have it out of your closet or wherever you keep it. I'd be right, wouldn't I?"

He kept his expression carefully blank. "You'd be right."

"And the job you had, the one I thought was so trivial, it had something to do with this cougar. Right?"

Kaler put the carbine on safety before settling next to her on the rock. "It's no big deal."

"Tell me."

He should have known she would push him hard. The truth had always been important to Leigh. To him, too, although he had a feeling she would find that hard to believe.

"The cougar is crippled. Seems to have lost some toes on its rear left foot, probably to a trap. Because it can't hunt properly, it's taken to raiding some of the outlying farms."

"Successfully, I assume."

Kaler watched the sunlight play over her face. Her skin was pale, and her mouth was tense.

"So far it's managed to kill a couple of sheep and a Doberman. A group of orchardists from the co-op hired me to put the poor bastard out of its misery."

Kaler watched some of the color return to her face and prayed she wouldn't ask any more questions. When she sighed heavily and then smiled, he almost shouted in relief.

"Poor Guntar," she mused softly. "He's a sorry excuse for a man, but he did sort of seem to care about his dog." She straightened her shoulders, smoothed her shirt and got to her feet. "Well, so much for Leigh's bout of hysterics. I didn't mean . . . *oh my God!*"

Her hand flew to her mouth. She was staring fixedly at the tracks he had already examined. "Kaler? Those are the same tracks . . . Father's and Danny's. The cougar's after them now, isn't it?"

"Remember what I told you once? Never jump to conclusions. Let the evidence lead you there."

Her gaze followed the tracks as far as she could see. "What do you call that if it isn't evidence?"

"First of all, I'm not sure those prints were made by your father and son, and secondly, until we check it out, we don't know what that damn cat is doing."

Leigh gave him an impatient look. She wasn't buying, or perhaps he just wasn't good at selling.

"Seems to me this co-op is going to a great deal of trouble, hiring an expert like you, just to shoot a crippled mountain lion that's killed a couple of sheep. Why doesn't one of those ranchers just shoot it himself?"

"Mountain lions are protected." He took great care to keep even the slightest hint of his own sharpened concern out of his tone. "To shoot one, you have to get a permit from Fish and Game."

"A permit I doubt they would issue just because a rare and endangered mountain lion was bothering sheep. Seems to me they'd sedate it and set it free someplace far away instead."

"Let it go, Leigh," he warned. She was pushing him into a corner, and, like the cat he was hunting, he hated blind corners.

"No, I need to know the truth. I can handle anything if I know the truth."

Kaler scowled, feeling more and more like the cocky five-year-old who'd lied to his mama and hadn't been able to sit for a week. He'd never lied again. Not unless a person considered telling Mendoza he was going to die if he didn't turn state's evidence a lie. And Leigh most definitely did.

Shifting the Winchester from his right hand to his left, he gripped her arm and urged her away from the marks in the dirt. She jerked her arm from his grasp and planted both feet securely.

"I'm not taking another step until you tell what you're hiding."

She wouldn't, either, he thought, and he wasn't in the mood to fight her.

"You want the truth. Here it is. The cat has to be killed because it's already savaged a four-year-old girl in her own backyard and ripped her father pretty good when he tried to save her."

"You mean she...died?" Leigh asked in a hollow voice.

"No, but she's going to need a lot of plastic surgery."

She seemed so fragile suddenly, and yet he knew that she wouldn't break, not the way he'd broken. No one would ever find Leigh dead drunk in a gutter. For all her ladylike ways, Leigh had more guts than he ever had.

"Then of course, you...have to kill the cougar. Before he finds Danny and Father."

"Leigh, a big cat only hunts when he's hungry. Right now his belly is full. He won't be hunting for another twenty-four hours, maybe longer."

"That doesn't seem all that long, does it?"

He decided that the best remedy was activity. "In that case, I'd better get to it." He shoved the Winchester into her hands, forcing her to take it.

"Careful, it's loaded." Before she could protest, he turned and jogged toward the place where they'd left the packs.

Leigh slowly extended her leg and tried not to wince at the pain shooting through her calf muscles. Next to her, Kaler slept with his back turned toward her, his breathing deep and measured.

The ache in her muscles increased until she had to move or suffer a painful cramp. Slowly and silently she eased into a sitting position.

"What's the matter?" She heard the rustle of movement, two hundred pounds of hard muscle and sinew turning from one side to the other.

"I keep thinking about Daniel. If anything should happen to him..." Her voice caught, and she bit her lip.

"If he's like his mom, he can handle whatever happens."

The dark seemed to close in, making her uneasy. Nervously she plucked at the edge of her sleeping bag and wondered how long before the first fingers of dawn reached into the tent.

"I keep remembering Guntar's dog when he came charging down that hill at us. It's hard to image him being...ripped apart like that." She took a slow breath and willed calm into her voice. "I keep telling myself that Guntar has already found the cat and shot him."

"Very possibly."

"Is he a good shot?"

"Better than most."

"As good as you?"

Kaler's hesitation was slight, but all the more noticeable because of the dark. "Some say he's better."

"Why did you beat him up when you were kids?"

Suddenly the air felt different, almost electric, as though the lightning of last night had suddenly returned. She struggled to see his face, but the darkness was too thick, adding to the sixth sense warning her of approaching danger.

"He called my mother a whore. I broke his jaw."

Leigh gasped. "How old were you?"

"Eight. He was ten." His voice took on an edge. "I saw the look on your face when you got a good look at him."

"You could be brothers," she admitted softly. "You even have the same name."

"Max's father's name. Giving me that name, too, was Patrick Kaler's idea of penance for my mother. She was pregnant when he married her, pregnant by Patrick's best friend. His already married best friend. Good old Max Guntar. She claimed that she was raped one night after a harvest party."

"Did Patrick believe her?"

"Who knows? He married her, and he never spoke to Max Guntar, again."

"You grew up knowing all this?"

"Everyone knew. All my brothers and sisters had dark hair and eyes. I stuck out like neon, with my blond hair and blue eyes. When I was still younger than Daniel, I remember asking God every night when I said my prayers to make me look like everyone else. It never worked."

"What about your mother?"

Kaler felt a rush of emotion, most of it painful. The helpless rage was long gone, but the pain it masked was still there. He carefully tamped it down until he felt only a distant empathy for the stoic, raw-boned woman. "She spent the rest of her life being grateful that Patrick had saved her from disgrace."

Leigh hugged her legs closer to her body. "Why didn't you ever tell me this before?" she asked softly.

"It didn't seem necessary."

"And now?"

"You're a beautiful, sexy woman, Leigh. You're bound to marry again, maybe even have more children. What then? Will Daniel grow up feeling as though he has to be better and stronger and smarter than everyone else, just to justify his damn existence?"

"Never," she whispered fervently. "Danny's the most important thing in my life, and he knows it. He'll always know that."

She heard him move and recognized the sound of fabric sliding over bare skin. A split second later she heard a soft hiss, followed by the sudden glare of the propane lantern.

He was lying on his side on top of his sleeping bag, wearing gray sweatpants worn so thin they did little to hide the muscular contours of his thighs and buttocks. His chest was bare.

The harsh light shadowed his face and added a mesmerizing depth to his eyes. His jaw was whisker dark, and his hair was disheveled. Cords stood out on his neck where it was braced on his hand.

"What happens when he grows up and learns to count?"

"Count?"

"Yeah, months. As in the difference between your wedding anniversary and his birthday."

Leigh suddenly felt sick inside. "I'll tell him the truth."

"The same as you told me, right?"

There was nothing in his voice to send shivers down her spine, nothing in his expression to send her pulse racing, nothing but a mild curiosity.

"I wish I hadn't."

"Why not? It's true, isn't it? You wouldn't lie about something like that just to get my help, would you?"

"Is that what you think?" she asked with a sudden catch in her voice. His eyes darkened, and his jaw tensed, as though he were waiting for more. When she remained silent, he merely shrugged.

"It would be a hell of an irony if you were, wouldn't it? You stopped loving me because I broke a few rules to bring down the cartel. Telling a man he's a father when he isn't, sure as hell breaks all the rules I know of. What did you call it seven years ago? Shameful and dishonorable?"

She flinched. "You're right. It would be dishonorable."

She would have turned away, but his hand suddenly came up to cup her chin, preventing her from escaping. "I didn't mean to bring that up again."

"Yes, you did. And you meant to hurt me, too. Does it make you feel better?"

Kaler fixed his gaze on the pride-stiff line of her slender shoulders. He was ashamed of himself, and that added fuel to his smoldering anger.

"What do you expect? You come busting into my life again, stir up things I've worked hard to bury and then tell me I have a six-year-old son I've never seen. By my thinking, I have a right to be upset."

She drew a shaky breath. "To be upset, yes. Not deliberately cruel."

"You're right," he said, rubbing his belly. "I'm out of line."

"I understand. This is . . . stressful for both of us."

"Stressful, hell! It's like seven years never happened. I see you and I want you, and I'm mad as hell about that, if you want to know the truth."

"That's just sex. . . ." Her voice faded as his fingers slid along her neck. The tips were rough, the palms callused and warmly intimate.

"And you want me, too, don't you?" His thumb slowly brushed the curve of her jaw as his gaze roamed her face, making it difficult for her to concentrate.

"I don't even know you anymore."

"You don't have to know me to want me. You wanted me that first day in my office, and you didn't know me then."

"That's not true."

"A guy like me learns to read people's eyes real quick. I saw what was in yours that day. A little fear, the usual female wariness and a whole lot of sexual fascination."

She raised her lashes and looked into his face. Tension rimmed his mouth and tightened his jaw. His eyes were very dark, as though the shadows had taken over completely.

Part of the night sky seemed trapped in his eyes as he let them rest on her face, and yet there was purpose there, too, the kind that had her automatically on guard.

"You weren't like any man I'd ever met. Maybe that's why I couldn't seem to make my usual defenses work against you."

"I never had any defense at all against you. That's what scared me. It still scares me."

Leigh was suddenly aware of the silence of the night. "Kaler, I . . ." She paused to wet suddenly dry lips. "If we made love, I might get pregnant."

To her surprise, he seemed startled, as though he hadn't even given such a possibility a thought. "I wish you would."

"But you . . . you said you didn't want children."

His eyes took on a dark sheen. "It looks as though Mother Nature knew better, doesn't it?"

"We're not in love anymore," she whispered past a sudden sharp ache in her throat.

Something shifted in his expression and then was gone, leaving his blue eyes smoked with desire.

He removed his hand from her back, only to use it to brush back her hair. "Belle told me once that nothing in this world ever happens by accident—not even a baby. Maybe Danny was God's way of giving us a second chance."

He angled his mouth over hers in the lightest of kisses. "I've missed you, Hank. Like holy hell."

She felt his enveloping warmth first and then the rough silk smoothness of his mouth on hers again. Her lashes fluttered closed, and her mouth trembled.

"Kaler, please . . ."

"If you're worried, I'll make sure you're protected. I promise."

Instantly his mouth firmed, taking hers over and over like a man who'd been hungry for too long. She, too, found herself responding like a starving woman, reveling in the hard pressure of his mouth and the fiery rasp of his breathing.

Her fingers sought the strong lines of his neck, loving the masculine feel of his skin and the provocative texture of his thick hair.

She inched closer until the tips of her breasts touched his chest. Sensation rushed through Kaler's body like a river overflowing its banks. He fought for control, but feelings pushed at him from all sides, distracting him.

"Sweet," Kaler murmured against her mouth. "And wild, like high mountain honey."

He slid his mouth to the fragile curve of her neck. Beneath her warm smooth skin, her pulse fluttered wildly against his lips. It was still there, that quick rush of pride whenever he felt her catching fire for him.

Still pressing small kisses against her throat, he eased her back against the thick padding of her sleeping bag. Her perfume clung to the soft inner lining, enveloping him.

The pleasure that shimmered through him approached pain in its intensity, driving him closer to the edge of his will. Hunger rippled and shifted inside him. He told himself that wanting was different than loving. Safer. Easier to control.

The heat inside him grew, escaping through his pores to bead on his skin. Suddenly the fleece of her sweatshirt seemed frustratingly thick and constricting. He leaned toward her and used his hands to push her shirt to her shoulders. Her breasts gleamed white, drawing his gaze. Dark circles, puckered from desire, framed nipples as hard and perfect as precious pearls.

Opening his mouth, he tested the tiny erection with his tongue. She shivered, and at the same time arched back her head, eager for more. His breath caught as a fiery sensation of raw need ran through him. His groin grew hot and heavy with pooling blood.

"Your breasts are fuller."

Her lips softened and parted. "From nursing Danny."

Kaler cursed the too-vivid imagination that had him seeing her smiling lovingly at a tiny boy child suckling from one of those perfect breasts.

He kissed the thin silver lines left from that time, and as he did, it came to him that he would have sold his soul to have been there for her. To have held her hand when the pain was at its worst. To have asked her forgiveness for failing her.

"Tell me what you want," he whispered hoarsely.

"Touch me," she pleaded feverishly, her eyes drowsy with desire.

Kaler slid his hand to her breast and cupped it in his palm. "Here?"

"Yes, oh, yes!"

He squeezed slowly, wringing a moan from her softly parted lips. Beneath his palm, her nipple quivered in answer to some inner response she couldn't control.

"You like that?"

She moaned and arched upward to press her soft flesh harder against his hand. To his surprise, his hand trembled. He flattened his fingers and let them run along her rib cage to the ribbed band of her shorts.

Her skin was impossibly soft beneath the fabric he pushed lower and lower until her thighs were fully exposed, enticing him to caress every inch with his mouth. Small shudders took her, bringing a thickness to his throat and a painful fullness to his body where the blood pulsed against his distended flesh.

Her skin was almost translucent in the dim light, and her eyes glowed with an inner fire. Feelings he had ruthlessly denied for seven years threatened to swamp him. His body screaming for release, he kissed her belly, then feathered his fingers lower and lower.

Gritting his teeth, he took his pleasure in watching the expressions chasing across her face. Tension first, then helpless desire, and, finally, surprise as his fingers fondled the small hard nub buried intimately in the silky hair and moist flesh.

Suddenly she arched and bucked, then buried her face against his shoulder as the tension burst. His hand stilled, and he let her clutch and tear at his hair, his neck, his shoulders, until she slowly, lazily relaxed. But he wasn't finished.

She was silk and cream and heat against his fingers, an utterly feminine creature of feeling and sensation. Her lashes flew upward, and her mouth opened in a silent plea.

He felt the small ripples, then a violent convulsion quickly escalating into a hard spasm against his fingers. Gasping and quivering, she fell backward, a drowsy sated smile curving her lips.

Kaler withdrew his hand and tidied her clothes before lying down on his side next to her, his head braced on his hand.

Slowly, like a woman floating lazily on a warm wave, she lifted one hand to his face. "A man of many talents," she murmured tenderly as her fingers traced his mouth.

"Most of which are damn rusty," he muttered before kissing her fingertips.

"I was afraid I'd never see you smile like that again," she murmured.

"Like what?" he asked indulgently before turning her hand so that he could kiss her warm, throbbing wrist.

Kaler was momentarily startled. How could he feel good when he was about to explode with unslaked hunger? he thought, and then realized that she was right. He was hurting, but he was also high as a kite because he'd given her pleasure.

"I'd better watch myself around you," he murmured as he drew her closer. "You know me too well." A man was vulnerable when a woman knew him better than he knew himself.

"Why didn't you?" she asked softly, and her voice was thick with tender concern, the kind that cut into him. He raised his gaze to hers and found her watching him with a liquid urgency.

"You were worried about consequences. This way there aren't any."

Not for her, she thought as she kissed his chin and then his mouth. She was feeling wonderfully relaxed and deliciously feminine, but he was lying there tense as a bowstring and hurting.

"Dear Kaler," she murmured. "So tough on the outside and so wonderfully sweet on the inside."

"Don't go fitting me for any halos," he muttered. "I've got enough on my conscience as it is."

"Maybe we both do."

"Any idea where that leaves us?"

"No, and right now I don't want to think about anything but this minute and how good I feel."

Leigh wet her lips, firing a spark in his mesmerizing eyes, but the shadow remained. It came to her then, in the swift sure way of a startling, irrefutable truth, that Kaler was a man who needed desperately to be loved. Not for his skills or his courage or his strength, but for himself, the way he should have been loved years and years ago.

"Kiss me again," she whispered. "Like you used to when—" She tried to take a breath, only to have it turn ragged and needy. Kaler groaned like a man in agonizing, unrelenting pain before his mouth settled over hers again.

His skin was hot and damp where her fingers clutched his shoulders, hotter still where the chest hair curled tightly over his heart. The texture beneath her touch were familiar and arousing—the smoothness of skin, the slice of a scar from some long-forgotten battle, the pebble-hardness of tiny male nipples half hidden by sweat-slick hair, the ridged tautness of his belly.

Her hands trembled as they worked the sweatpants over his hips. They trembled more as they touched hot distended flesh and thick tightly coiled hair. His loins contracted in violent, involuntary spasms, and he groaned again.

"My turn," she whispered hoarsely between kisses.

Kaler inhaled violently before trapping her hand with his and moving it to his belly. His gaze searched hers intently as though he were looking for an answer to a terribly important question.

"You don't have to—" His voice ended in a groan as she freed her hand and began stroking him with the same care he'd used on her.

"Feel good?"

"Yes. Yes!" he managed through clenched teeth. His skin was stretched taut and hot against her palm.

When she bent over him, her mouth warm and moist on his throbbing flesh, he lost the little control he had left. His release came violently, wrenching a guttural, primitive groan from his stiff lips. A tremor ran through him, seizing the last of his energy, and he was lost.

Seven

The tent had taken on the eerie gray of predawn when Leigh woke. She was curled against Kaler's chest with one hand clasped in his.

Wind whispered through the thick branches overhead, and the air seeping around the edges of the tent flap was cool and pine scented.

Leigh closed her eyes and breathed in the familiar warmth of his skin. It felt so good to be close to him again. So right. No one had ever made her feel as safe and protected as he had. Or as feminine.

Perhaps because he himself was so masculine. And so strong. As a man he was irresistible in the way that immense power is invariably irresistible. And strong in the way a man of the land is strong.

His brawny hands and arms were those of a day laborer, sinewy and muscular from constant use. And his legs had the look of great power and endurance, especially the calves, which bulged even when he was relaxed.

There were scars, too—low on one hip where enemy shrapnel had sliced to the bone. Some were jagged where the hot metal had ripped away his flesh, others were straight and precise, where a navy surgeon had cut into the wounds to remove the sharp metal and then worked to rebuild his shattered pelvis.

It still gave him pain sometimes, she knew, and there had been times after a long trip on horseback into the Sonora Desert when he'd limped for days. No one offered sympathy. No one had dared.

Very slowly she raised her head and looked into his face. He was sleeping deeply, his mouth slightly parted and relaxed.

Such a beautiful mouth, she thought with a drowsy smile. Strongly formed, with just a hint of humor lurking at the corners, and an intensely masculine shape to go with his intensely masculine face. She had loved his mouth from that electric moment when she'd first experienced the shock of his sudden grin.

The last of his boyhood was in that grin, perhaps even the last of his innocence. It had beguiled and intrigued her, even as it had gone deep inside to excite her.

A diamond in the rough, she'd thought then. Uneducated, but brilliant. A man who knew his own strengths and relied on them without having to prove anything to anyone, and yet capable of endearing shyness when it came to women.

Leigh slowly ran her gaze along the aggressive line of his jaw. He'd turned a fiery red the first time she'd undressed him and then kissed his strong, scarred body inch by slow inch, and when she'd whispered how much she loved him, he'd trembled.

Emotion gathered in her chest until she felt it pound in rhythm with her heart. He was a man who was understanding of the failings of others and yet brutally unforgiving of his own.

There was an old saying, something about hating the sin but loving the sinner. It was possible, she realized. No, more than possible. She loved this man.

Tears collected in her eyes and constricted her throat. Forgive me for demanding perfection in you when I'm so far from perfect myself, she thought as she slowly touched her mouth to his.

His eyes flew open, then narrowed. "Is it morning already?" He blinked, struggling toward the kind of alertness that was usually second nature.

"Yes, sleepyhead. Don't tell me I wore you out?"

"Since you're the only woman here, it must have been you."

His arm curled around her until she was drawn tight against him. The downy hair of his arms and legs did little to soften the hard contours of bone and muscular sinew crushing her soft flesh. "It's been a long time since someone woke me with a kiss."

"How long?" she asked, then blushed.

"About seven years." She blinked, clearly disbelieving, and he chuckled.

"Your poker face is slipping, Hank." He nuzzled her hair away from her neck and kissed the warm skin he found there. Her pulse leapt, then raced under his mouth.

"It's none of my business," she murmured, arching her neck.

"No, it's not," he whispered against her fragile throat. "Just as the things you did with your husband are none of mine."

His breath was warm on her breasts as he bent to kiss the still swollen tips. Heat rushed through her to pool low in her belly. As though sensing her body's surrender, he used his tongue to taste one nipple and then the other.

"Feel good?" he whispered against her swelling flesh.

She moaned, suddenly unable to form the right words. It couldn't happen again, she told herself, or tried to, but her body was busy answering an age-old instinct, softening inside, growing moist, preparing to welcome the seed that only a man could provide. A daughter this time, she thought in some unprotected part of her heart.

"That's it, honey. Put your arms around me. Let me feel your breasts against my chest. Let me feel . . ." His words ended in an indrawn hiss as he slid into her warmth a few inches, then withdrew.

His hand slid between them to caress the spot where his arousal had tantalized her. Shivers of need raced across her belly, leaving her flesh quivering helplessly.

"Me, too, honey," Kaler whispered as his fingers slowly tormented her. His kisses were drugging, and his hands were gentle yet skillful as they touched her in achingly familiar ways, ways that he himself had discovered first.

Leigh writhed, trying to draw him closer. Instead, he took her to the brink over and over, drawing back when her moans became frenzied. Leigh clutched his arms, his shoulders, his arms again, trying to draw him into her.

His mouth replaced his hand, and she cried out at the searing pleasure of his tongue flicking the hot moist nub, already sensitized and throbbing.

She cried out at the moment of release, her hands clenching reflexively in his thick hair. She was wild with wanting even as she shuddered helplessly.

Tugging on his hair, she urged his head up until his teeth gently nipped the now distended mound between her legs.

"Fill me," she whispered in husky supplication. "I need to feel you."

"Are you sure?"

"Yes, now. Please."

His body shuddered as he raised himself over her. His dark face was contorted with need, his eyes midnight blue from wanting.

He thrust into her quickly, and she gasped, a long raspy thread of sound. His hands were almost savage in their exploration of her body, his mouth opening over hers to allow his tongue to plunge deeply.

He moved like a man driven by a need beyond his control, plunging over and over in an age-old rhythm. His savagery was new, startling her at first, then exhilarating her as she realized he was making love to her like a man who had denied himself this kind of physical pleasure for a long, long time.

She wound her arms around his neck and let her mouth cling to his as she answered his thrusts with quick arching movements of her hips, matching his frenzied movements with her own.

At the moment of release he cried out her name with a desperation that pushed her over the edge into an explosion of sensation and feeling and emotion.

Afterward they lay spent and silent, their damp bodies still joined. Kaler's eyes were closed, and his deep even breathing told her that he was sleeping again.

Leigh eased from his arms and sat up. Her body was deliciously relaxed, and her breasts were still flushed from the bloom of sexual excitement. Inside, she felt twinges of a new and intimate soreness where he had filled her over and over.

Smiling, she pressed her hand against the fullest curve of her belly, wondering if even now a part of Kaler and a part of her were joining to create life.

Her heart gave a little flutter, then a larger one as reality sank in. A baby. Kaler's baby.

. . . God's way of giving us a second chance.

The words hung in her mind as she awkwardly slipped into her clothes in the tiny space. As she tucked her shirt into the waistband of her jeans, she tried to imagine Kaler changing diapers with his big rough hands and singing lullabies in that raspy baritone more suited for intimidating wrongdoers. The image wouldn't gel, leaving her feeling sad and on edge as she slipped from the tent and headed toward the bushes.

Where the hell was she? Kaler asked himself as he jerked his shirt over his head. Didn't she know better than to wander around alone at dawn with a renegade cougar on the prowl?

With one eye on the rumpled sleeping bag on Leigh's side of the tent, he dressed rapidly in clean skivvies and the same rumpled shorts he'd stripped off the night before.

Always a light sleeper, he rarely required more than five hours to feel rested; he couldn't remember the last time he'd slept past sun up. Nor the last time a woman had left his bed without his knowing it.

Barefoot and grumpy, he emerged from the tent to a glorious sunrise and the tempting scent of strong coffee. Leigh was crouched over the fire, forking slices of canned ham into a skillet. She had dressed for the cooler weather in jeans that hugged her small trim fanny in all the right places and a pale gold T-shirt that did great things for her tan, not to mention the way it draped provocatively over her breasts.

"Good morning," she called huskily as their eyes met. Hers were soft. His suddenly stung. From the wind and the smoke, he told himself.

"You should have poked me. I don't like you wandering around by yourself."

Leigh smiled at the frustrated growl, but inside she had gone all warm and soft. The man had been alone too long. He needed a lot of tending. A lot of loving.

"Don't worry. You would have heard me yelling at the first sign of trouble."

"If a cougar's close enough to spot, it's too late for yelling." He propped his rifle within arm's length before joining her.

Leigh repressed a shiver. "I'll remember that."

"You'd damn well better."

Leigh used a folded towel to lift the coffeepot, and she poured him a cup. "I made it extra strong."

Kaler grunted his thanks before gulping it down. Strong didn't begin to describe it. He cleared his throat, but the bitter taste remained.

"I figure we'll head west, toward Elk Peak." He kept his tone businesslike and his expression neutral. He hadn't felt so tongue-tied and awkward since he'd been sixteen and full of raging hormones.

"Elk Peak? Is there a camping area there?" As Leigh's gaze returned to his, he saw the sated softness disappear. For a moment she had forgotten why they were there, but he hadn't. He couldn't afford the luxury. Not when he'd discovered just how susceptible he was to a woman he'd been determined to slice out of his life forever.

"No campground. In fact, it's pretty wild."

"Then why—"

"The trees are thick there, and there's plenty of water, just the place for Bigfoot to make his home."

Leigh's jaw dropped. "You're serious, aren't you?"

"Absolutely. If your father offered to take your son on a proper search for Sasquatch, that's where he'd head. The bastard's a snob, but he keeps his word."

"I—Is that a compliment or an insult?"

"Can't you tell?"

"Not with you. Not anymore."

She wasn't wearing makeup, and her face was pale, with the exception of the rosy whisker burn along the curve of one cheek. "Did I do that?" he asked as he trailed his finger lightly over her skin.

"I think we both did." She let him see her intention in her eyes before she flattened one palm against his rough whiskers.

"Are you sorry?" Though he spoke softly, his voice carried an edge.

"No, not sorry. Apprehensive, perhaps."

"About the possibility of pregnancy?"

In the bright daylight, his words seemed terribly clinical—unlike last night, when he'd seemed almost wistful about fathering a child.

"I'd be lying if I said I wasn't." She let her hand fall away from his face and her attention return to the skillet.

Kaler grasped her shoulders and turned her to face him again. "Leigh, I admit I have a lot to work through about us, past and present, but one thing I know for sure. Nothing in this world would please me more than to see you pregnant with my child."

He brushed his mouth over hers, arousing her and moving her deeply at the same time. Tears collected behind her closed lids, wetting her lashes. Kaler used his thumb to wipe them away before kissing her again.

"Hold that thought," he said gruffly before he headed past her toward the stream, the closest thing to a cold shower he could find in the mountains.

There was a lot he should have said, he thought as he sluiced cool water over his head and shoulders. Words a woman deserved to hear from a man who'd just made love to her twice in less than twelve hours. Words a mother deserved to hear from the father of her son. Words he had a gut feeling he would never be able to say.

Four hours later, Leigh neatly folded the waxed paper that had contained the granola bars and dried fruit they'd eaten for lunch and stowed them with the other trash in a compartment of her pack.

A few feet away, Kaler was sitting with his back to a bleached rock, one arm resting on his raised knee. Wind swirling upward from the canyon below ruffled his hair, and his eyes were crinkled at the corners as he stared straight ahead, but he seemed oblivious to the glorious vista spread out below them.

The sun had been high overhead when they'd stopped in a grassy spot overlooking the river valley below. Elk Peak was directly ahead, its stiletto tip still covered with snow.

"It's amazing how cold the wind can be up here," she said as she drew the tied sleeves of her sweatshirt closer to her neck.

"Blame it on the ice pack. In the old days, icemen used to haul chunks down from the peak in sleds, then transfer them to horse-drawn wagons."

"It's still gorgeous, cold wind or not. I can see why you came back here."

Kaler trailed his gaze over the shadow-dark spikes of fir and pine on the distant horizon. "My brother Andy always claimed it was magical up here. Swore it was haunted.''

''By whom?''

''Indians, mostly. He swore he could see their ghosts, especially at twilight.''

''Did you ever see them?''

''Not the kind Andy meant.''

Leigh hugged her knees close to her chest. ''When I was a little girl, I had this walk-in closet in my room, and Mama Sarah, my nanny, used to call it a 'sin closet.' She said that every time I was bad, I let a bad spirit out of that closet to haunt me.'' She shook her head. ''There was a time when my room felt awfully crowded!''

Kaler chuckled. ''Hell, there wouldn't have been any room at all in mine.''

She grinned. ''I bet you were something when you were a kid.''

He'd never been a kid, not in the way she meant. By the time he was Dan's age, he'd already learned to pull his own weight and stay out of Patrick's way.

''What about Dan?'' he asked. ''Does he have a 'sin closet,' too?''

''No, but that doesn't mean he doesn't get himself into mischief, especially lately.'' Her face softened into a smile. ''He was a perfect baby, rarely cried, kept to an easy schedule. My friends couldn't believe how happy he was all the time.''

''What happened?''

She shrugged. ''I wish I knew. Sometimes I think he just woke up one morning and decided to drive his mother crazy.''

''Is he succeeding?''

''Not yet, but most days I barely hold my own, especially when I get called to his school by the principal for a 'friendly chat.'" She sighed. "It seems that darling Daniel has a pugnacious streak, especially when the kids tease him."

Kaler made a fist and stared at the familiar pattern of veins and sinew. "Sounds like someone should teach the kid to box."

Are you volunteering? Leigh nearly asked, then thought better of it. The subject of Daniel still lay like an unexploded bomb between them.

"I'm afraid that would only make it worse," she said ruefully. "At the moment he only picks on kids his own size. Heaven help us if he decides to tackle the big kids."

"Might teach him a lesson if he did."

"Maybe." Leigh looked up in time to see a pained look come and go in his eyes. "What about you? Did you have trouble in school?"

It was a stab in the dark, but his sudden frown told her that she'd hit a sensitive target. "I had a bad temper when I was a kid. Back then, the big guys in school used to bait me, get me to attack so they could beat the tar out of me. I remember once, when I was six or seven, I ended up unconscious in about three feet of snow. Damn near froze to death before my mother found me. After that, I made sure I'd never lose a fight again." He glanced up to find her watching him. "Not with my fists, anyway."

"You taught yourself to box?"

"To fight," he corrected. "The marines taught me to box."

"How old were you?"

"Eighteen by then. I had this colonel come and talk to me after one of my fights. Wanted me to volunteer for this secret, elite force he was forming. Said I fit the profile they wanted."

"Profile of what?"

"I asked the same question. He hemmed and hawed and threw a lot of words at me, but it all came down to one thing. Legalized murder. Assassination. He said I had the instinct for it. Claimed he could see it in my eyes when I fought."

Leigh drew a deep breath. Perhaps once, a long time ago, she might have been skeptical. Now she knew better. Such things had been done during the Vietnam War, and, some said, were even being done today. "Did you accept his offer?"

"No, but I wanted to."

Kaler slowly opened his hand and studied the thick knuckles and prominent veins. He'd touched his share of women over the years, but his body remembered only hers. He'd never allowed himself to wonder why. Now he knew. Loving Leigh, being loved in return, was the closest he'd ever come to belonging.

"You're not a cold-blooded killer," she said with a low throb of conviction. "If you were, you would have taken Mendoza into a dark alley and put a bullet in his head."

Kaler glanced at the rifle lying within easy reach. "Believe me, I thought about it. Sometimes I think it would have been easier that way."

She scooted closer, and he let her put her arms around his waist, but his expression remained remote. He had learned to live with his guilt and pain. He hadn't learned to forgive himself for being human.

His thumb slowly brushed the curve of her jaw as his gaze roamed her face. "I wish I'd never heard of Gilberto Mendoza," she said fervently.

"So do I," he muttered before lowering his head. His arms came around her waist so violently, she was nearly bent in two. Pressed so tightly, she felt his need in the roped tautness of his thighs and the steel of his embrace.

The wind, noticeably stronger now, snatched at their hair and tore at their clothes. Leigh clung tighter, trying to warm the bitter chill in Kaler's soul.

His mouth took hers over and over, until the desperate need gradually softened into tenderness and the hard knots torturing his muscles eased.

He lifted his head slowly, his eyes still a deep blue and his face flushed. Her fingers stroked his cheek, and she smiled at the stubble beginning to darken his jaw even though the day wasn't even half over.

"Hurts, doesn't it?" he asked in a raw tone.

"What?"

His smile was suddenly very gentle. "Guilt."

"Yes," she murmured as she scrambled to her feet and reached for her pack. "It hurts."

Eight

The footprints that had been so easily followed in the soft ground had all but disappeared when they reached a rock plateau overlooking the deepest part of Icicle Canyon. For the past hour, Kaler had been crisscrossing the hard ground, looking for signs that only he could see. He'd finally found a faint irregularity in a patch of sparse grass on the far edge.

"Is it Father and Daniel?" Leigh asked anxiously.

Kaler ran his hand over the flattened grass. "No, these are animal tracks."

Leigh fought a moment of crushing disappointment. "The cougar?"

"Yeah. See the difference in the depth of the tracks? He comes down more heavily on his crippled paw." He measured the distance between the hind and forepaws with his eye. Nine feet from nose to tail, he guessed. One of the biggest ever in the valley.

"Are the tracks fresh?"

He shook his head. "The ground was slightly damp when these tracks were made. From dew would be my guess, and that means early morning, before the sun dried the ground."

"*This* morning, do you think?"

"Possibly, though I doubt it."

"So, we keep heading for Elk Peak." She turned halfway around and shaded her eyes, searching for the snow-capped cone that had become a lifeline.

Oh, baby, I'm coming, she told her son silently, then squeezed her eyes shut. Danny is just fine and having the time of his life, she told herself fervently. Father is fine, too, or he will be, once I get him to the doctor.

Kaler saw the fragile slant of her shoulders as they pushed back bravely, prepared to take up her heavy pack again. He had a feeling she would take on the cat with her bare hands if it so much as looked at her little boy.

Love had a way of putting that kind of single-minded determination into a person. It also had a way of tearing a person to pieces when it wasn't returned. Abruptly he stood and brushed the trail dust from his hands.

"We follow the cat."

"But you said we were close. Wouldn't it make more sense to—"

Kaler cut her off. "If your father is camped in these parts, we'll find him. In the meantime, we follow the cat."

The cougar might not be able to hunt in the usual way, but he still had all his senses. If there were other humans within a five-mile radius, a hungry cat would find them.

"But—"

"One problem at a time, Leigh. A renegade cat with a taste for human blood is as dangerous as any aneurysm."

Leigh's stomach quivered, but she managed to keep her terror from her tone. "I see your point."

Kaler kicked himself for being an idiot. Hurting her wasn't the way to keep her from worrying herself sick.

"Aw, hell," he muttered, pulling her into his arms. He held her close, feeling the shivers shaking her small body as though they could no longer be controlled. Her arms slid around his waist, and she held on tight.

"I'm so scared," she said, her face pressed against his wrinkled, sweat-stained shirt, as though she couldn't quite get close enough.

"I know, honey." His voice was rough, not because he didn't care, but because he felt helpless, the way he'd felt that morning in Da Nang when he'd gotten the word about Andy.

"You're doing your best," she said, as though speaking her thoughts aloud. "You have to think about...about other children, too, like that little girl playing in her own backyard."

Suddenly she was swallowing repeatedly, trying to choke down the tears. But it was no use. She started to cry, each sob shaking her body more violently.

Kaler shot a quick look around, spied a spot of dense shade and scooped Leigh into his arms. She gasped, but he stopped her protest with a quick hard kiss. By the time she could breathe again, he had them both settled on the grass with his back to the rough trunk of a Douglas fir and the carbine propped nearby.

"Kaler—"

"Shh." He kissed her wet cheek before tucking her head into his shoulder. "Now have your cry, and make it a good one, while you're at it."

"I never cry. It's so tacky...." She choked on a sob, drawing a brief smile from Kaler as he smoothed her hair with one rough hand.

"Make an exception, then." He stared at the jagged horizon and murmured words that he'd once used to soothe his brothers and sisters when they came running to him with some hurt or other.

She felt so small in his arms, so utterly feminine and sweet, with her skin incongruously perfumed and her frizzing hair crackling with static electricity under his palm.

A man should protect the ones he cared about. He should stand tall and be strong and have all the answers, the way he'd once thought he'd had them for his trusting little brother.

Damn, he thought, squeezing his eyes shut against the sudden tears. He'd had all the answers, all right, and Andy had died. When he'd tried to make sure other kids like him didn't end up six feet under, too, he'd made a royal mess of it.

Never again, he vowed. No more making decisions for anyone but himself. He couldn't take the pain when he screwed up, he told himself as Leigh slowly pulled out of his arms and wiped her eyes on the bandanna she'd appropriated a day or two back.

"My poor mama would have a hissy-fit if she saw me now," she said before blowing her nose.

Kaler drew back and inspected her with a severe look. "I'll say. No decent lady should look as sexy as you do with swollen eyes and a blotchy face."

She swatted him, but her eyes softened. "I keep telling myself everything will be all right if I can just stay calm," she murmured, smoothing the tear-blotched cotton over his shoulder. "It always works in the office, but some-how... out here... I'm sorry."

His smile was achingly gentle, but instead of erasing the lines in his face, it somehow seemed to deepen them.

"Yeah, so am I, sorry I messed up seven years ago and blew what we had all to hell."

"That's in the past."

"No, it's not. I wish it was."

"If you'd only told me about Andy, I would have un-derstood."

"Maybe, but that doesn't make what I did right. I would have sacrificed a man's life because I made the decision he didn't deserve to live, not a judge and jury."

"You did your best."

"That's the point, isn't it? My best wasn't good enough."

This time he didn't wait for her to move. He hoisted her off his lap into the rough grass, then reached out and pulled her to her feet. At the same time he heard a quiet footfall to his left and whirled, his rifle already in his hand.

"Whoa, Kale! Don't get antsy."

It was Guntar, standing a dozen yards away, his hands spread. The Remington was still slung over his shoulder, the lens of the scope flashing in the sunlight.

Kaler slipped his finger from the trigger as he pointed the carbine's barrel skyward. "Been wondering about you, Max. Sorry about Bullet."

Pain flashed in the other man's eyes, and Leigh sensed that Kaler's half brother had truly loved his dog, no mat-ter how cruelly he'd treated the animal.

"So am I, Mr. Guntar," she said, drawing a sharp look from Guntar's cavernous eyes.

"We were partners, ol' Bullet and me. Saved my life more'n once, he did." His face went slack for an instant, his eyes losing focus, before he seemed to remember where he was. "He didn't deserve dying like that."

"No, he didn't. No one does."

Guntar's eyes went dead cold, wiping away even a trace of humanity. "That's where you're wrong." He shifted his gaze to the carbine resting easily against Kaler's shoulder and then to Kaler's face. "That cat's mine. Agreed?"

"Depends."

Guntar's mouth twitched. "If you're worried about the six thousand the co-op already paid you, you can keep it. Just give me the cat and I won't say a word."

"I don't take money I don't earn."

"Yeah, I remember them high principles of yours," he said with a sneer. "Went off to be some kind of war hero and never came back."

Kaler glanced down the trail. The very wildness and isolation of this place made negotiating with Max tricky. Especially with Leigh standing only a few feet away. Perhaps she didn't understand the danger she was in, but he did. Max had killed before to get what he wanted. He might again.

"Give me your word to make the kill cleanly," he told his half brother calmly as though he held all the chips, "and you can have the cat."

Guntar thrust out his jaw. "No way! That damned cougar's gonna wish it had never been born before I get done with it. A man ain't a man if he don't avenge a wrong to him or his."

"One shot, Max, in the heart or in the head. I want your word."

"*You* want?" Guntar turned a furious red. "Who gave you the right to give me orders?"

Kaler walked forward, his movements fluid and sure. When he was close enough he took something from his breast pocket and stuffed it into Guntar's. It was Bullet's collar.

"Bullet died doing what you trained him to do—attack. The cougar fought back and won. He doesn't deserve to be slaughtered for defending himself." His words were clipped, his tone chilling, rocking Guntar back a step before the big man made himself hold his ground.

"If it was your dog that got splattered all over them rocks, you wouldn't be talking like this!"

"I'd be hurting just like you are, and nothing would stop me until I made sure the cat was dead, but not for revenge. Take my word for it. You're only wasting your time if you think cold-blooded slaughter will help."

Guntar's eyes flashed an anguished blue and his big hands became fists. "Damn it, Kale. *I want that cat!* I need to put Bullet to rest."

Kaler understood that need all too well. "One shot, Max. A clean kill. Give me your word and the cat is yours."

Guntar uncurled one fist and thrust his hand forward. "You have my word."

The two men shook hands, and Guntar turned to leave. He got as far as the divided track when he suddenly stopped and turned back. "About that old man and a boy? I seen 'em this morning about four miles due south. 'Peared to be setting up camp."

Without waiting for an acknowledgment, he turned toward the track and broke into a jog toward the southwest.

Joy swept through Leigh like wildfire, bringing a shaky smile that slowly faded. "Why didn't he try to use that information, maybe trade it for the cougar?" she asked.

Kaler allowed himself a brief smile. In another lifetime he and Max might have been friends. "In his own twisted way, Max is an honorable man. Trading blood for blood is fair. Using the living as a bargaining chip isn't."

"You mean he would have told us about Father and Daniel even if you hadn't agreed to let him make the kill?"

"Yeah, he would have told us." Kaler slipped his Winchester over his shoulder and walked toward their packs. Leigh followed, silent now. Thinking. Evaluating and ultimately, he suspected, not really understanding this world where he felt so at home.

Instead of lessening with time and experience, the differences between them had only gotten more insurmountable over the past years. Without speaking, he helped her into her pack, then shrugged into his own.

"C'mon, Mama. Let's go find that kid of yours and his turkey of a grandfather." His hand was gentle as he tucked a stray lock of hair into her baseball cap.

She gripped his wrist, drawing his gaze to her face. "Kaler, about Danny—"

"Don't worry, honey. I'm not going to muscle into the kid's life or yours."

"But—"

"There's more to being a parent than biology, Leigh. We both know that." He used the back of his hand to nudge her chin higher, then kissed her lingeringly before he turned away.

"There, about ten yards left of that outcropping of rock." Kaler pointed with his binoculars before handing them to Leigh.

Late-afternoon shadows slanted across the clearing, striping the emerald grass and making it difficult to discern more than light and shadow in the distance.

Impatient and tired, Leigh stared at the spot Kaler had indicated. Her shoulders ached from carrying the heavy pack now leaning against Kaler's at their feet, and her legs were rubbery from the steady climbing.

"You mean that cloud?" she asked testily as she fine-tuned the focus.

"It's not a cloud. It's smoke."

"Smoke?" She frowned and narrowed her gaze against the eyepieces. "You mean . . . I see puffs. Smoke signals!" Rising up to disappear into the snowy slope of Elk Peak.

"Look below. See that flash of red."

"No . . . wait. Now I . . . oh my God, Kaler, you found them!"

"With a lot of help from Max."

"Forget Max. You would have found them without his help."

She threw her arms around him with a ferocity that nearly sent them both sprawling before he managed to brace both feet on solid granite.

"Father and Daniel are safe!" she cried softly, caught between joy and relief.

"Looks that way," he said, staring down into her shining eyes. In the sunlight they were shot with gold, and her lashes cast intriguing shadows on her cheeks.

His arms came around her, and his head lowered. He wasn't sure who made the first move, but suddenly her lips were against his.

Because the need was so strong to crush her against him, to savage her mouth so thoroughly that she would never want to leave him, he fought to keep his kiss gentle and his touch undemanding.

He had forgotten how quickly Leigh could fire his desire, even when he was determined to keep himself under rigid control. She was doing that now, with her hands warm on his face and her breasts soft and warm against his chest.

With his hands he tilted her head further and kissed her over and over until they were both flushed and breathing hard.

"End of the road, Hank. I'm going to miss you snuggled up next to me."

She went still, except for her mouth, which trembled ever so slightly. He kissed her until the trembling stopped, then lifted his head a few inches until he could see her face. He read both confusion and gratitude in the soft, shimmering eyes that had once ripped him with their disdain. He refused to look deeper.

"I don't know how to thank you. If it weren't for you . . ." Her voice choked.

Pressure built in his chest, like the sudden ache of a deep grief. His hands weren't as steady as they should be as he ruffled her hair into a dark frame for her face.

"No speeches, Hank. Let's just say I owed you one, and leave it at that."

The campsite was swept clean of debris, and the fire had been set within the safety of a ring of stones. A few yards away, still within the cleared area, a red three-man tent had been pitched in the shelter of a boulder large enough to serve as a barrier against the always unpredictable north wind.

A ramrod straight, silver-haired man sporting a Washington Redskins cap and a sturdy flaxen-haired boy wearing shorts and a T-shirt from Georgetown were hunched over a roaring campfire, using a towel to make puffs from the smoke.

Kaler stopped at the edge of the campsite and let Leigh walk the last few yards alone. Her father saw her first, and Kaler watched the man's polite curiosity give way to surprise and then delight. At a low word from his grandfather, the boy whirled quickly. His face lit up, giving Kaler a glimpse of a smaller, more masculine version of Leigh.

"Mommy, Mommy!" the youngster shouted as he dropped his end of the towel and took off running.

Leigh dropped to her knees and let the sturdy little boy hurtle headlong into her arms. Closing her eyes, she fought to keep from frightening him with her tears.

"Baby," she whispered as she breathed in the familiar little-boy scent. "I've missed you so much."

"Me, too, Mommy."

"Have you been having fun with Granddaddy?"

"Lots and lots, only we haven't found Bigfoot yet, have we, Granddaddy?"

"Not yet, but we still have ten days."

Leigh and her father exchanged warm looks. "So you decided to take your vacation with us after all," he said pleasantly, but his sharp gaze was questioning.

"Not exactly."

The ambassador's eyebrows disappeared under the bill of his cap. "Hmm, sounds mysterious, but it'll have to wait until after dinner."

"Yeah, we're having hot dogs al fresco," Daniel added as he snuck a quick look in Kaler's direction. "Who's that man with the gun, Mommy?"

Leigh curled her arm loosely around his waist and forced a smile. "That's Mr. Kaler. He helped me find you and Granddaddy."

"Why does he have a gun?"

"To keep us all safe in case Bigfoot doesn't like us poking around in his territory," she said in a mock-scary voice.

"Oh, *Mom!*"

Leigh snatched at the opportunity to give her son another bear hug before getting to her feet. "Father, you remember Max Kaler?"

Bradbury's gaze swung to Kaler's face. The frigid dislike was still there, tempered now by a reluctant curiosity. The old man might have retired and gained a few pounds around the middle, Kaler decided, but Ambassador Bradbury was still a pompous snob.

"Mr. Ambassador."

"I would be lying if I said you were welcome here," Leigh's father said in the same upper-class drawl Kaler remembered.

"Be lying myself if I said I was happy to be here," Kaler returned with a grin that lit a fire in the old man's pale eyes.

"Behave yourself, both of you," Leigh muttered before introducing him to her son. "This is Daniel."

Kaler nodded toward the boy, who was watching him with bright blue eyes. "Would you really shoot someone with your gun?" Daniel asked solemnly.

"Not unless I had to."

"Mr. Kaler's a guide and a tracker, darling," Leigh interjected quickly. "He knows all about the mountains."

"Me 'n' Granddaddy are hunting Bigfoot," Daniel said with little-boy gusto. "I bet you've seen lots and lots of his footprints."

"Not yet. How about you? Have you found any signs?"

Daniel's brow furrowed. "There was this funny growling sound last night. Close to the tent, too. Granddaddy said it might be Bigfoot come to check us out."

"What kind of a growling sound?"

"A Bigfoot growling sound." Daniel's chin lifted stubbornly. "Ask Granddaddy. Soon as we heard it, he built up the fire real big so we could get a better look."

Kaler pinned Leigh's old man with a hard look. "See anything special?"

Bradbury's expression was still frigid as he shook his head. "Fire probably scared it away."

Kaler gave the area a closer look. Bradbury knew his stuff, he would give him that. In the small clearing there was no thick brush where a cat could hide, no low overhanging branches or boulders. Pebbly ground that would crunch under a large animal's weight.

"Looks safe enough," he said, and the old man stiffened.

"I'm not an amateur, Mr. Kaler."

Leigh shot Kaler a sharp look. He didn't need words to know what she was thinking. "You'll stay the night?"

"Yes." Her question and Kaler's answer earned her a swift look of disapproval from her father, but Leigh was beyond caring. She had seen the bloody carcass beside the trail. He hadn't.

"I don't know about you men, but I'm so hungry I could eat the bark off that Douglas fir over there," she said with a smile for her son, who was clearly fascinated with the big, tough, rifle-toting stranger. As she'd intended, Daniel shifted his attention to the tree in question.

"I bet it tastes yucky."

"You're right. I'll make stew to go along with those al fresco hot dogs."

Daniel made a face, and Leigh burst out laughing. "Okay, okay, your comment is duly noted." Her gaze somehow ended up meshed with Kaler's. She saw wariness there and . . . nervousness.

Her heart gave a slow lurch. "Daniel, why don't you help Mr. Kaler put up his tent? Maybe that'll help you work up an appetite."

The little boy's chest puffed out. "I can put up Granddad's all by myself."

As Leigh watched the two of them walk away together, the enormity of what she'd done hit her. Kaler and Daniel were finally face-to-face.

"I imagine you have a reason for being with that man again?" her father said in a low voice. She jerked her gaze to his face. Disapproval was written in every line.

"Of course, I have a reason, and I'd appreciate it if you wouldn't call him 'that man.'"

Bradbury's shrewd eyes narrowed. "He's no good, Leigh. He'll only hurt you again."

"I hurt him just as badly."

Bradbury scoffed openly. "You did exactly the right thing. The man was a disgrace to himself and his country."

Leigh's temper flared. "He had one of the finest records in the history of the customs service."

"Which he soiled by acting dishonorably."

It was impossible to be angry with her father for using almost the exact words she'd once used and meant. How had she ever dared be so self-righteous? she wondered sadly.

"I wouldn't be so quick to judge him if I were you, Father," she said with a bittersweet smile. "Kaler and I are more alike than you know."

Nine

———

Kaler stripped off his shirt and used it to wipe the sweat from his face before throwing it to the grass. Flexing his shoulders, he took up his hand ax again and tested the edge with his thumb.

"Mommy says I shouldn't ever touch sharp things."

Daniel handed him another chunk of dead pine, then stepped back the way Kaler had taught him. Since they'd finished putting up the tent, the boy had stuck to Kaler's heels like a shadow. At first it had made him nervous. Now he realized he had come to like the company.

"Mommy's right. At least, not until someone's shown you how to be careful."

"Did someone teach you?"

"No, and I bloodied a few fingers before I learned, too." Kaler brought the ax down hard, splintering the soft pine into kindling, which Daniel instantly added to the rapidly growing pile.

"I wish I was as strong as you, Mr. Kaler."

"You will be someday."

"Mommy needs me to open jars sometimes, and sometimes I help her carry in groceries. She says I'm her best help around the house."

"I'll bet you are."

Daniel fiddled with a pinecone he was methodically pulling to pieces, and Kaler noticed that the small, stubby fingers were never still. The kid was a lot like Andy had been at that age.

"My daddy died when I was just a little kid."

It took Kaler a moment to make the connection—no daddy to help his mommy. A man would have to stay on his toes to keep up with this kid. "That must have been rough."

Daniel shrugged. "I don't 'member him much. Mommy said he loved me a lot, but he got real sick and had a heart attack and the doctors couldn't make him better." He turned his curious gaze on Kaler and frowned. "Did you know my daddy, Mr. Kaler?"

"No, Dan, I didn't. But I'm sure he was a fine man. Your mother wouldn't have married him unless he was."

Daniel bobbed his head. "She said I should always be proud because my name is Pinchot and a lot of important people will know who my daddy was. And Granddaddy says that a person's an . . . ancestors are very important."

Kaler brought the ax down so hard his wrist seemed to vibrate. "Your granddad's absolutely right. Family is very important."

Daniel drew back and heaved the cone toward a nearby holly bush. It thwacked against something solid, and the bush exploded in a flutter of wings and a fury of angry birdcalls.

"Good arm," Kaler said with a quick nod. "Nice curve to that cone, too."

Daniel eyes brightened, then faded. "I always get picked last when we play ball at recess."

"Why's that?" Kaler decided that he'd split enough wood for one night's fire and sheathed his ax.

"I can't hit," the boy admitted glumly. "Mommy tried to teach me, but she's worse than I am."

Kaler found himself intrigued with an image of Leigh crouched over the plate with a baseball bat slung over her shoulder. He could almost see the small frown of concentration between her silky eyebrows and the smooth expanse of thigh below her shorts.

"Maybe Mommy needs somebody to teach her."

"She says bad words to the ball when she thinks I can't hear."

"Next time she does that, haul her into the bathroom and wash her mouth out with soap."

Daniel looked startled, and then, as he thought over the advice, gleeful. "Is that what your mommy did when you were bad?"

"Sometimes." And sometimes she'd had to resort to harsher measures to get her message across. He'd never been one to change his mind easily once it was made up.

"I like that," Daniel said, grinning. "She's got this stupid pink soap in her bathroom. I bet it tastes rotten!"

"Don't even think about it, Daniel Pinchot!"

Leigh's shadow fell between them, eerily elongated by the lingering rays of the sun. Kaler found his heart accelerating at the sound of her voice.

He glanced up quickly, but in his mind his gaze was taking a more leisurely route—up the slender length of denim-sheathed legs to the curve of her hip and then to the soft full breasts only partially camouflaged by the baggy gold shirt.

"Uh-oh," he said to her son. "I think Mommy's just busted us."

Daniel giggled at his mother's stern expression. "I'm gonna tell Granddaddy about the soap." He ran off, leaving a cloud of dust behind.

"I see Danny's been telling tales about me," Leigh said as she came closer.

"A few."

No matter what he was doing, he was acutely aware of her. It wasn't a conscious thing, nor was it something he could change, and it set him on edge, like the scream of a cougar caught in a trap.

Even when he'd been letting Daniel order him around like a pint-sized drill sergeant as they'd put up the tent, he'd been noticing the quick, anxious looks she kept sending his way. Mama Bear was looking after her cub and worried sick that he might get hurt.

Kaler wanted to tell her that the boy was safe with him, that he would take care of him, but he knew better. He'd tried to take care of Andy once, hadn't he?

"I told Father about the aneurysm while you and Daniel were collecting wood," she said before giving a quick glance over her shoulder.

"How did he take it?"

"Stoically. He agrees with me that he shouldn't take chances and suggested we start back tomorrow."

"Shouldn't take more than three days of easy walking."

"Downhill, thank goodness."

"Too bad we didn't need to call in the chopper. The ambassador would love arriving at Seattle General in style."

Kaler stacked lengths of pine in the crook of one arm and carried the wood to the fire ring. Leigh did the same.

"Can I help?" she asked as she watched him feed the flames until they were good and hot and ready to sear hot dogs or anything else that came too close.

Kaler brushed bits of bark from his arm and grinned. "How about scrounging up a hot bath and a cold beer?"

"I'm terribly sorry, sir," she drawled in her deepest Southern accent. "We're fresh out of beer and bathtubs. How about a bucket of water and Kool-Aid instead?"

"Only if you serve it the same way you served me Dom Pérignon for my birthday one year."

Her gaze went straight to his navel before she could stop herself. She blushed to the tips of her ears, before shooting him a reproachful look.

"Did anyone ever tell you that you play dirty?"

He saw her eyes soften as he came closer. "Games are for kids who have time to play them, Leigh. I don't."

He ran the flat of his palm down her bare arm and thought about the feel of her cuddled next to him in the warm cozy tent. It had been a long time since he'd wakened feeling so good about life. And about himself. It was a hell of a feeling, one that he hadn't had for a long time, and it scared him.

"Don't look at me like that," she whispered as she tried to tidy the tumble of hair brushing his eyebrows. Her touch was so gentle it tempted a man to read more into it than he should.

"Like what?"

"Like you wish I'd never walked into Belle's five days ago."

"I do."

"I...see." she tried to turn away, but he shot out a hand to stop her. "Things were under control then. I had as much work as I could handle, and a few friends, and now and then I'd meet a woman who didn't want more than I wanted to give. It was enough, or so I thought."

"And now?"

He stared at the stark white peaks and thought about living the rest of his life alone. "And now it's not, but that's not your fault. It's mine."

He felt her draw a quick breath and then push against his chest until she could get a look at his face. He relaxed his hold but kept his arms around her.

"Kaler, listen to me. What you said about second chances—"

"Mommy? Were you really kissing Mr. Kaler?" Daniel and the ambassador were standing nearby. The old man had a strong grip on his grandson's hand, and his expression was stern.

Leigh's gaze whipped sideways, and her smile had a frustrated tilt. "Yes, darling, and right now we're having a very important conversation."

Her gaze swung to her father's face and held. At the same time Kaler felt her fingers tighten around his forearm, and he knew she was telling him without words that she wasn't ashamed to be discovered in his arms.

But he knew that couldn't last. Not when they were off his mountain and back in the real world. So did her old man, he thought as their gazes collided.

"Sorry to interrupt," Bradbury said with a stiff scowl that said just the opposite, "but it's time to get the hot dogs going if we're going to eat before dark."

"We're having Snickers bars for dessert!" Daniel exclaimed. "Granddad said so. 'Cause it's a special occasion."

Leigh groaned. "And milk, I hope."

Daniel's pleasure dimmed. "Yeah, but it's the yucky powdered kind. And we already ran out of cocoa."

"Well, we *are* roughing it," Leigh told him with a quick grin.

Kaler stepped away from the possessive tug of her fingers and tried to ignore the eager looks Daniel kept sending his way. "I need to take a quick look around before the light goes. I'll be back."

"I'll go with you," Daniel proposed quickly, pulling away from his grandfather and hurrying to Kaler's side. "Maybe we'll see Bigfoot."

Kaler felt a thud somewhere below his heart. "Not this time, Dan," he said as gently as he could manage. "Stay here and help your mama. She needs your more than I do."

He walked away, but not before the flash of hurt in the boy's bright blue eyes nearly sent him to his knees.

After dinner Leigh volunteered to do the dishes, and the ambassador talked Daniel into a game of checkers in his tent where the light was better, leaving Kaler and Leigh alone by the fire.

Kaler had offered to help, but she'd turned him down. "Enjoy your coffee. You've already done more than your share of the work."

Now, as he sat on a flat rock on the other side of the fire, he noticed the tension shaping her mouth and the tiny lines furrowing her brow.

He'd expected those things. She was worried about her father, and it showed. And he'd also expected to find himself thinking about the tantalizing silk of her skin beneath her shirt and the fiery demand of her lips against his. He was a man, after all.

What he hadn't expected was the old emptiness nagging at him again. It wasn't hunger. He'd grown up with his belly empty more times than he wanted to remember. And it wasn't sexual craving, not in the usual sense, anyway. He wished like hell it was. From the time he was shaving regularly, he'd learned how to manage that kind of ache.

Irritated at himself, at her, at a situation that was beginning to wear badly on him, Kaler slugged down the last of his coffee and glared at the thick sludge in the bottom of his plastic cup.

"Is it that bad?" He glanced up to find Leigh standing in front of him with the coffeepot in her hand. Above her head the sky was turning from lilac to purple as the sun sank lower behind the peaks. "I was just about to offer you the last cup, but maybe I shouldn't."

"The problem's with me, not the coffee," he said before holding out his cup. She emptied the pot before settling next to him on the rock. Her skin was satin in the firelight, tempting Kaler to pull her onto his lap and bury his face against her throat.

"Leigh, about this afternoon...I didn't mean to hurt the boy's feelings. It just didn't seem like a good idea to let him get too used to me."

Away from the clearing a large boulder screened the tents from his sight, but Kaler could picture the kid and his grandfather bending over the board. No doubt the old bastard demanded the same perfection from Leigh's son as he'd demanded from her at that age. Some role model, Kaler thought, then reminded himself that Daniel's future was none of his business.

"Don't worry, Kaler. Daniel's surprisingly resilient."

Leigh watched his hands curving around his coffee cup. He had strong hands, capable of the greatest tenderness or the coldest violence.

"Kids usually are."

"Were you?"

"Obviously."

Not so obviously, she thought. He still had deep scars from the time she'd come to think of as his bad years. She snuck a look at his profile. It was hard as granite in the firelight.

"Danny still likes you," she said as she put the pot on the ground. "Whether you want him to or not."

"He's a lot like Andy. Has the same curiosity and... innocence about him."

"And that bothers you?"

He hesitated, his cup halfway to his mouth. "Yeah, it bothers me."

"Why?"

Kaler scowled. "What kind of question is that?"

"An honest one."

"A damn silly one for a Georgetown Phi Beta Kappa, don't you think?"

"It won't work, Kaler. I'm on to you now. Every time the conversation gets too personal, you start a fight."

"The hell I do!" He threw his coffee into the fire, where it created a violent hiss of sparks, before tossing the cup into the dishwater.

He was on his feet before Leigh could stop him and striding into the darkness before she could make her legs work. Darkness closed around her as she followed the sound of his footsteps.

Ahead in the distance, she saw the white blur of Kaler's shirt and then the dark shapes of low-hanging branches. She ducked, but she wasn't fast enough and something snagged her hair.

"Ouch!" Caught, she tugged at the stubborn twigs, trying to free herself.

"For a smart woman, you can be damn stupid," Kaler grated as he turned back to help her.

"Silly *and* stupid," she muttered. "No wonder I can't balance my checkbook."

His fingers pushed hers aside impatiently, and she expected pain, but his touch was surprisingly careful as he worked to get her untangled.

"There, you're free. Now turn around and head back to the campfire where you belong before I take you to the ground right here and make love to you."

"I wish you would, since that's the only time you let me see the man I fell in love with."

"That was a long time ago."

"Yes, all of forty-eight hours, give or take a few odd minutes."

That rocked him back like a quick left jab, but he recovered quickly. "Bull. You'd fall in love with any halfway presentable guy who managed to find your old man and your kid. Shrinks and cops have that happening to them all the time."

"What difference does it make to you what I feel or don't feel?" she challenged.

"None," he grated, but his hands were already threading in the freshly washed silk of her hair.

Kaler had promised himself that he wasn't going to touch her. His head was already unsettled enough, but he'd forgotten that the woman he called Hank could tempt a saint to forget all the good and valid reasons why he should just walk away.

Valid, hell. Not when her arms were around his neck anyway, and his thigh was sliding between hers.

One last time, he told himself. In memory of everything he wished he had done right with her.

He kissed her mouth first, taking his time, letting himself memorize the taste and feel of her soft lips. And then he treated himself to a feast of kisses down the side of her neck before recapturing her mouth.

The past two nights had told him that she still liked long, languid kisses, the kind that left both of them breathless, and he gladly indulged her. And she liked to have him rub her nipples ever so slowly with his chest, something that made him almost as hot as it made her.

Her nails lightly scraped his scalp, forcing a groan of pleasure from his mouth into hers, and he realized that she knew a few things about him, too.

His hand cupped her breast and found it swollen beneath the pebbly nipple. Her shirt was some thin material, but not thin enough to allow skin to feel skin. Frustrated, he pushed it high enough so that he could stroke the bare skin beneath the skimpy silk of her bra. At the same time he rubbed his thigh against hers, his body screaming with each slow, intimate stroke.

Crickets chirped nearby as he lifted her into his arms and carried her to a dark patch of grass. He wanted her with a violence that had his head spinning and his knees about to give way.

He let her down slowly, gently, until her feet touched the ground. Her hands clutched at his arms, and she swayed, her eyelashes fluttering and her mouth soft and moist.

"Hold me," she murmured shakily. "I... There seems to be a problem with my knees."

"Tell me about it," Kaler replied, his voice raspy and his own balance precarious. "Even when I was doing my damnedest to blame you for my mistakes, you had a hook so deep in me I couldn't blast it out with booze or exhaustion or other women."

Her gaze faltered at that, and she would have looked away, but he held her chin, trapping her. "My gutsy little Hank," he murmured. "I can't seem to stop wanting you." His gaze searched hers intently, as though he were looking for the answer to a terribly important question.

"I can't seem to stop wanting you, either."

Her hands trembled as they worked the buttons of his shirt, then pushed it from his shoulders. They trembled more as they unbuckled his belt and slipped free the top button of his jeans.

He groaned, stopping her before she could do more. "My turn," he whispered hoarsely between kisses.

When he drew her down to the cool damp grass, she went willingly, her body quivering and her knees weak. "Easy, honey," he soothed.

When he had her naked, he ran his hands over her reverently, remapping the curves and swells of her breasts, her waist, her belly.

Kaler felt the spasms rippling the satin skin beneath his hand and gritted his teeth against the fiery heat engorging his flesh. Trapped against the unyielding thickness of denim, his body pulsed and strained, eager to be sheathed where his fingers were rhythmically stroking.

Her soft, desperate moans were more exciting than the most explicit words, driving him to the edge of his control. He tried to think of other things—the cougar, planting pear trees, winter blizzards. But all he really wanted was Leigh, the feel and taste and sweetness of her, and the balm of her laughter.

He fought for control, fought to keep from easing his violent need in a few swift hard strokes. He began to shake, his need as much emotional as it was physical, perhaps more. Much, much more. For her smiles, her laughter, her sweetness. Her trust.

His touch, the feel of his hand on her soft thighs, was more than she could bear. Her hands brushed the hard ridge behind his fly, then worked the zipper. His harsh breathing shuddered into a groan as her fingers found warm, rigid flesh.

Eagerly she rose over him and guided him to her. He arched his neck and dug his fingers into the thick grass, struggling to accommodate her rhythm.

Slowly, and then more quickly, he felt the small ripples take her, then a violent convulsion quickly escalating into a fiery explosion deep inside.

He arched upward, letting go in a rush. He soothed her then, stroking her gently with fingers that still shook and murmuring gentle words that no other woman had ever heard.

He drew her to him and covered her with his shirt. She murmured his name on a deep sigh before nestling closer, and he moved until his spent flesh was cradled against her slick moistness. It felt so good to hold her like this. To feel her hair tickling his chin and her breasts pressed against his chest.

"It's getting late, and we don't have a blanket," he said, when his heartbeat was back to normal. After tonight, he would keep his vow not to touch her, no matter what it cost him. "We'd better get back before the ambassador comes after me with my own gun."

"I am thirty-seven years old, you know," she murmured before kissing his shoulder.

"The man still considers me one notch lower than a cockroach."

"You have to admit, you haven't gone out of your way to win him over."

"Believe me, honey, that's not possible."

He felt her smile brush his neck. "Then I'll just have to put up with both of you the way you are."

His hand stilled, and he shifted his gaze to the branches overhead. "For three more days, yes," he said as he sat up and took her with him. His shirt puddled in her lap, and she shivered from the sudden chill.

"You're telling me not to expect more than this, is that it?" she asked carefully.

"You always were quick," he said, but the tender kiss he pressed against her mouth took the sting from his words. "We both know you're just wasting your time trying to find a reason to care about a beat-up ex-customs cop without a future." Kaler gathered her clothes and handed them to her before getting to his feet.

"I think you forgot the part where you tell me I'll thank you for saying these things some day," she said as she tugged her shirt over her head.

He told himself her voice was muffled from the cotton, not tears. "You will."

"Don't tell me what I will or will not do," she said tartly, standing on one foot and then the other to pull on her jeans. "And I don't need my father or you telling me what I should feel or not feel, either."

Kaler tucked in his shirt, zipped his jeans, then gripped her arms and held her motionless. "Right now, this minute, I want to ask you to marry me. More than anything in this world I want to go to bed beside you every night and wake up holding you the next morning. And I want to take care of you and your son. But I can't."

"Why not?" He caught the rush of surprise in her voice and realized that she had spoken before she'd thought.

"When you leave this mountain, you have a life to go back to. A career, people who are counting on you, a damn fine reputation, a son to be proud of, and you've earned it all." He knew his smile had a lopsided cast and wasn't all that convincing, but he did the best he could. "The best thing I can do for you and your son is stay the hell out of that life."

"Don't you understand? I love you. I've never—"

He stopped her before she could say things she would regret. He stopped her with a long, hard kiss. "I'll see you safely to the ranger station, and then we'll say goodbye like two old friends who live in different worlds and always will."

They returned to the campsite in silence. Leigh didn't know what to say, and Kaler knew he'd said it all.

Ten

Kaler added kindling to the still smoldering embers, along with a handful of dead grass, and waited for them to catch hold. Seconds later, flames were crackling loudly in the dawn silence.

He was the only one awake besides the small family of deer he'd glimpsed nibbling breakfast at the other end of the clearing. The morning was nippy, and the grass was dew damp and slippery. Hands on his hips, he stretched the kinks from his back, inhaling deeply of the crisp air. It tasted like autumn.

Wouldn't be long now before the trees turned and the dew turned to ice crystals, he thought. Another month, maybe less at this altitude. And then the winter would settle in, keeping him inside and trapped with his thoughts.

They would be of Leigh, he knew, and the precious few days they'd had in this place he loved. He would never again walk the mountains without feeling haunted by her smile. No matter how many hours a day he'd walk or how hard he'd push himself, he would be shadowed by his memories of her laughter and her grit and her fire. Hating the thought, he upended a slab of pine log and settled in front of the fire.

"What kind of a gun is that?"

Kaler saw the kid then, standing a few feet away, dressed in dark blue sweats and muddy sneakers with untied laces. His hair stood up in crazy blond spikes, and his eyes were bright. The boy was eager to be accepted, to be liked, exactly the way Kaler had been at six. And like himself at that age, Dan needed a father to give him confidence and courage to try new things. He just didn't need Kaler.

Kaler's face felt stiff as he forced a smile. "It's a Winchester Model 94 carbine."

Daniel's blue eyes rounded and radiated excitement. "Wow!" he exclaimed. "That sounds awesome."

"It's just a big name for a not so big gun. Sometimes I think Mr. Winchester wanted to scare the game more than he wanted to shoot it."

Daniel came forward, shoelaces slapping the ground with each step until they were as soaked as the grass. "I have a gun, and it's a lot bigger than yours. Mommy keeps it on the wall in her den."

That got Kaler's full attention. "On the wall?"

"Yeah, next to this funny-looking thing Granddaddy gave us. He said it's called a family tree...only it really looks like another dumb piece of fancy paper."

I hear you, kid, Kaler thought. His family had been too poor to care about amassing a formal history. Day-to-day survival was all that had mattered.

Daniel squatted next to him and reached for the small plastic bag Kaler had just taken from his pack. "What's this?"

"A cleaning rag."

Kaler took the bag from the boy's small hands and extracted the oily piece of chamois cloth. "Feel how soft it is? I use it to wipe down all the metal parts."

"Why?" Daniel asked after a moment's consideration.

"To keep rust from forming."

Daniel touched the chamois gingerly. Tactile sort of kid, Kaler thought. He'd been a toucher, too, when he was a kid. For a long time he thought nothing was real unless he could feel its weight and texture. Hell, maybe he still thought that.

"Is rust bad?" Daniel asked after a moment of deep thought.

"Bad enough, especially if the barrel should explode in my face."

Daniel sank to the ground and crossed his legs. A stranger would take them for father and son, Kaler thought, and then banished the thought. Daniel wasn't his son. He never could be.

"Mommy said I mustn't ever touch my gun until I'm twenty-one."

"The one on the wall?" Kaler had forgotten how convoluted a kid's mind could be.

"Yeah. Mommy says it's an antique." His small forehead furrowed, and his eyes became solemn. "That means it's worth lots and lots of money."

"So I've heard," Kaler replied with equal solemnity.

Daniel watched silently as Kaler's hands skimmed expertly over the blue steel, catching every spot of damp and speck of dust.

"Mr. Kaler?"

"Right here, Dan." He wondered what it would feel like to have a boy like Daniel call him "Dad." Pretty damn good, probably.

"Are those deer over there by those funny-looking trees?"

"Yes. They generally feed in the early morning or at dusk."

"They don't know we're here, do they?"

"Sure they do. See the one standing off to the side by himself? The one with the big rack."

"Rack?"

"Antlers." Seven points, at least, a magnificent trophy. He hoped it didn't end up in some bastard's den.

Daniel squinted, then nodded. "Is he the boss of the others?"

Smart kid, Kaler thought. Smarter than he'd been at that age. "Yeah, I guess you might say that. See the way he's sniffing the air and his tail is up in the air like a flag? He's watching us. If he senses danger, he'll give a signal, and the others will run for safety."

Daniel's head swiveled between the gun and the buck a few times, and Kaler could see the notion taking shape. "Have you ever killed a deer with your gun?"

"Yes, a long time ago." Kaler finished wiping down the carbine and returned the neatly folded rag to the bag.

"Could you still?"

"I could, but I won't." Kaler reached into his pocket for the bullets he'd just removed and slipped them one by one into the magazine. "I only hunted for meat for the table. Now I can afford to buy my food at the store."

Daniel's eyebrows drew together as he thought about that for a while. "But maybe you could put the antlers on your wall, like they did down at the store in town where Granddaddy bought groceries."

Kaler ran his hand over the rifle's barrel. He had once killed a buck on the run with one shot through the heart. His brothers and sisters had eaten for a week on the venison. Patrick Kaler had sold the rack to buy booze—to old man French at the general store in Cashmere. Kaler avoided looking at it whenever he shopped.

"Wouldn't it be better if this particular buck was around to look out for the mommas and babies?" he asked, watching Daniel's eyes. They were shaped like Leigh's and had her thick curly lashes. Only the color was different.

"I guess so." Daniel picked up a log and threw it onto the fire, then watched the flames shift and flare. "Maybe you could show me how to use an ax today."

"Maybe tonight." Kaler told himself that it wouldn't hurt to spend a little time with the boy, teach him a few things while he had the time. "If your mother says it's okay."

Daniel's face split into a grin. "Do you have a mommy and babies at your house, Mr. Kaler?"

"No, I live alone."

"How come you don't have any boys and girls like me?"

"Just not lucky, I guess." Kaler stood suddenly, and the buck bounded to the left, followed instantly by the does and their yearlings. I know how you feel, fella, he thought. If I had a family, I wouldn't let anyone hurt them, either.

Leigh leaned against a oak sapling and pointed her toes, stretching her still-sore calves. It was midmorning, and Kaler had called a break after two hours on the trail, ostensibly to let Daniel rest. But her father's face had been as pink as Daniel's and his breathing even more labored.

Slumped on a nearby rock, the ambassador was fanning himself with his hat and sending disapproving glances toward the tree-covered slope where Daniel and Kaler were crouched next to a dead tree stump.

"I thought Daniel would be disappointed to give up the search for Sasquatch, but your Mr. Kaler seems to have diverted his attention into other areas."

"He's not *my* anything, Father. He never was." She couldn't quite keep her pain out of her voice, and her father's head turned sharply, bringing to bear shrewd blue eyes that had invariably bored through her thickest armor.

"But you want him to be, I take it?"

"It doesn't seem to matter what I want. He thinks he's not good enough for me."

"I agree. He's everything a father fears in a man—rough-spoken, a bit too wild to tame, too willing to take dangerous chances. And he hurt you very badly once. I don't want you hurt again."

Leigh glanced down at the diamond band winking in the sunshine. Edward's ring. Someday she would give it to Daniel to pass on to his wife.

"He thinks you're against him because of his background."

"Perhaps I am, but only because I know how intimidating you can be, even to men whose backgrounds match yours. I was afraid Mr. Kaler would end up shooting you."

"Father!"

He patted her hand with a reserved man's clumsiness before releasing it. "Sorry, darling, but you always were a handful, especially after your mother died and I was left to deal with you alone."

Bradbury reached into his pack for his water bottle. He offered it to Leigh first, and when she refused, took a long swallow before saying calmly, "He could have kept his job at Customs. Did you know that?"

Her jaw dropped, and she slowly shook her head. "How do you... Of course. You and Director Carlton belong to the same squash club."

"Your Mr. Kaler was considered too valuable an asset to lose, and so he was offered a deal. Swear under oath that he was only bluffing when he told that man Mendoza he would sic his cartel buddies on him if he didn't talk and he could keep his position."

"But... but he told me himself that he wasn't bluffing. That he never bluffed."

"Exactly what he told Stu Carlton."

Leigh let her gaze rest for a long moment on Kaler's broad back. He had something in his hand, a beetle of some sort, and Daniel was poking it gingerly with a stubbly forefinger, his small body braced trustingly against Kaler's knee for balance.

The midmorning sun caught the metallic gold strands in Kaler's thick hair, turning them nearly as light as Daniel's.

"Father, remember what you told me once? That never, under any circumstances, does the end justify the means if those means are less than honorable?"

"I remember. I still believe that. And now I think, so does Kaler."

"Yes, I have a feeling that's exactly what he believes," Leigh said softly. "That's what makes it hurt so much."

Bradbury took his time stowing his bottle in the pack, then checked the straps before straightening. "If he's the man you want, go after him the way you've gone after everything else in your life."

"I tried, Father," she said. And she'd failed.

Daniel touched the disturbed ground with a grubby finger. Kneeling next to him, Kaler waited for the barrage of questions he knew was coming. It had become a pattern. Daniel asked questions, and he answered them.

"But how do you *know* a deer made this track?" Daniel demanded finally. Still pint-sized and already a skeptic, Kaler thought. The kid was already two steps ahead of the rest of the world.

"Deer and elk and even mountain goats walk in a special way that's easy to identify. See this sharp mark like a cut in the ground?" Kaler explained with more patience than he'd thought he possessed. "That's made by the deer's hoof. It's like he was walking on his toenails, only he doesn't have any."

Kaler glanced around until he spied a faint indentation in the grass halfway up a nearby rise. "C'mere, I'll show you something else," he said before getting to his feet.

"Show me what?" Daniel asked impatiently. Instead of answering, Kaler led the boy to the spot he'd noticed.

"See the way the grass is all flattened out in a kind of circle?" he asked when Daniel reached his side.

"Uh-huh."

Kaler knelt and beckoned Daniel to move closer. "You know how you sleep in a tent so you'll feel safe from the dark and the night animals?" he asked, and Daniel nodded.

"Well, a lot of animals in the wild sleep on a hill with their backs to the wind so that they can see what they can't smell and smell what they can't see. It's their way of feeling safe. Deer are like that."

Daniel looked impressed. "Do you know *everything* about wild animals'n' tracks'n' things?" he asked with a wide-eyed innocence that made Kaler sad inside when he saw it.

"Not everything, no. I know a lot of things because I grew up around here, just like you probably know a lot of things about your neighborhood in Phoenix."

Daniel brightened. "Lots and lots," he agreed. "I even know what to do if I see a rattler when I'm outside playing."

His expectant look told Kaler he was bursting to impart *his* knowledge this time. "What do you do when you spot a rattler?" Kaler asked without showing a hint of the amusement he was feeling.

"First you freeze," Daniel intoned gravely, "and then, when the rattler is nice'n' calm, you back up very, very slowly'n' then, when you're far enough away, you turn around and run home as fast as you can."

Kaler ruffled the boy's hair. "I'll remember that—if I ever run across a rattler."

Looking enormously pleased with himself, Daniel leaned against Kaler's knee and stared at the flattened grass while Kaler watched Leigh walking hurriedly toward him and wondered how long it would be this time before he stopped hurting.

"See any sign of Bigfoot?" she called.

Daniel's face brightened. "No, but Mr. Kaler knows everything about tracks and stuff. I bet we'll find him real soon."

"I hope so, darling," she said as she handed him a granola bar.

"Granddaddy always had Snickers for snacks," he grumbled, but he was already opening the sealed packet.

"Mommies serve granola. It's a rule." Her gaze shifted to Kaler's and held. "Any sign of Max?"

"No," he said as he got to his feet and shaded her with his body.

Leigh had been savoring the subtle longing in his eyes when he'd seen her. Now, suddenly, there was no expression, no interest at all, in his eyes. None.

"Mommy had a bad dream last night," Daniel confided.

Leigh threw her son a reproachful look, but it was too late. Daniel had already transferred his attention to the granola bar.

Kaler fought a fast battle with himself and lost. "What kind of bad dream?" he asked.

She shrugged. "Who can remember dreams?"

Kaler could. The ones with her in them, anyway. More than once he'd wished he couldn't.

"She was crying," Daniel amplified between bites.

Her gaze touched Kaler's only briefly, but it was long enough to give him a good look at the smudges under her eyes and the tiny lines around her mouth. He felt a soft thump inside, as though he'd just been kicked hard.

"I never wanted to hurt you, Hank."

"I know. I was just feeling sentimental, that's all. No big deal, as you—"

She was interrupted by two loud cracks in rapid succession.

"Gunshots!" she gasped.

"Damn straight they are! From a Remington."

Three more shots exploded. From the south, Leigh thought. "Guntar?"

"Undoubtedly." Kaler glanced around, then nodded toward Daniel. "Stay here, and for God's sake, hang on to the boy."

Daniel started to follow, but Leigh caught the back of his shirt and held on. "Wait! I'm coming with you!" she shouted. But Kaler was already running.

"Mommy! I want to go with Mr. Kaler!" Daniel yelled, struggling to pull free.

"What's wrong? I heard shots!" the ambassador shouted as he hurried toward them.

"I'll explain later!" she shouted back before crouching in front of her son and holding him tightly by both arms. "Daniel, I need you to stay here and protect Granddad, okay?"

"But Mr. Kaler might need me."

"Granddad needs you more." She shot a quick glance at her father, who nodded as he rested a hand on Daniel's shoulder.

"Mommy's right, Daniel. Your old granddad needs you to stay with him here." Daniel looked disappointed but resigned.

"I'll be back," she promised before sprinting after Kaler. He was already out of sight, but his long, powerful strides and size-twelve boots had left deep gouges in the loose soil.

It seemed like hours but had to be less than five minutes when she spied him ahead, standing next to a wind-twisted juniper.

She called his name and he turned. His jaw was set, and his eyes were like flint.

"What . . . ?" she managed to gasp out between painful breaths when she reached his side. Before Kaler could answer, a flash of red to her right caught her eye. It was blood pooling beneath the severed neck of the largest mountain lion she'd ever seen.

It was a magnificent male, with a lush, shiny coat in various shades of tan, ranging from the darker golden color of its broad back to the delicate pale tan of its belly. Its hindquarters were thick with muscle and sinew, designed for speed and power, while the forepaws, smaller and more agile, were tipped with long, lethal claws. One hind leg, however, was deformed and laced with scars, and the huge paw was missing two toes.

"Oh my God," she cried softly. "That poor animal." Her stomach heaved, and she bit down hard on her lower lip. She looked away quickly and found that Kaler was watching her.

"Guntar?" she asked.

"Yeah, one shot in the heart, just as he promised. I never thought to tell him not to take the head."

"Kaler, you can't be responsible for everyone and everything. It's not your fault that you credited him with more good traits than he has."

Kaler's narrowed gaze made another circuit of the surrounding area. She saw him pause, then concentrate on a small cluster of craggy rocks near a wooded area fifty feet or so eastward.

"Do you see something?" She found herself whispering and her eyes straining.

He cocked his head and scowled. "Hear that? Sounds like whimpering."

Leigh held her breath, but all she heard was the rush of the wind. Disappointed, she shook her head. "No..." She heard it then, a faint mewling sound coming from the cluster of rocks.

"Max?"

"Possibly." Frowning, she managed another quick look at the mutilated body. The blood was already congealing, and the thick tan fur had lost its luster. Damn you, Max, she thought angrily.

Kaler quickly cocked the carbine and checked the wind. "Stay here, and this time I mean *here*."

She didn't need to take another look at the lion's long sharp claws to know that he wasn't issuing the order out of some macho caprice.

"Be careful," she whispered, trying to smile.

"Always."

He moved upwind, moving with the powerful, oiled grace of the cat he was stalking.

Leigh edged away from the carcass, also staying upwind and taking care to move silently. Even though she wanted to keep her gaze riveted on the comforting breadth of Kaler's big back, she kept her eyes moving, looking for possible danger.

It seemed like forever but was in reality only a minute or two before Kaler froze, prepared to take aim. Leigh stopped in midstride and waited, scarcely breathing. Suddenly he was lowering the rifle and beckoning her closer.

"What is it?" she whispered when she reached his side.

Instead of answering, he directed her gaze toward a cavelike hole fashioned by a long-ago tumble of jagged boulders. Inside, curled into a pale gold ball of fur and four enormous paws, was the cutest cub Leigh had ever seen.

"Well, hi there, baby," she crooned softly. "Aren't you precious?"

The cub mewed and got to its feet. Like a domestic kitten, its tail went up and it trotted toward Leigh eagerly. She moved forward, but Kaler stopped her.

"But he's lonely," she murmured, aching to cuddle the furry baby in her arms.

"If you contaminate the den or his hide with your scent, the female might not come back."

"You're right. I didn't think," she said as she quickly hopped onto a waist-high rock, out of reach of the lonely cub. More determined than ever, the cougar baby prowled below, its cries more demanding.

"Where do you think mama's gone?" she asked when she couldn't stand it any longer.

"No way of knowing for sure. Hunting, maybe, although that's unlikely. This cub looks too small to have been weaned yet." She saw that he had pulled his finger from the trigger, but the safety remained off.

"I heard five shots, at least. Maybe Guntar got her, too."

"If he did, where's the carcass?" He hesitated, then handed her the rifle. It had a balanced feel in her hands and smelled of oil and gunpowder. "If mama comes back and sees you, she'll come at you with everything she has."

Leigh nodded. "I hope she doesn't."

"Max didn't have time to get too far. I'm going to look around, see if I can spot him."

He skirted the den, then angled north, his gaze fixed on the ground in front of him. Twice he knelt and ran his fingers over the pebbly earth, and then he was screened from Leigh's sight by a stand of pine.

By that time the cub had both front paws stretched as high as it could reach, trying every way it could think of to climb onto the rock where she was waiting. Twin stripes of black fur ran like frown lines between his big ears, and his head looked too heavy for his tiny body, reminding her of a stuffed lion Daniel had had as a baby.

"I know," she murmured. "You're scared and hungry and lonely, and I wish I could help, sweetie. I really do."

Mewing impatiently and twitching his tail furiously, the cub tried leaping onto the rock, but it wasn't quite big enough to manage and ended up in a growling heap.

"Determined little thing, aren't you?" Leigh said with a laugh. "You and Danny would get along just fine."

Sensing a sudden movement to her left, she raised the rifle and curled her finger around the trigger. It was Kaler, returning alone, a scowl on his face.

"What?" she asked, lowering the rifle.

"We've got a problem."

"Guntar?"

He nodded. "Yeah, and another set of cat tracks."

"Mama Cougar." Leigh glanced toward the prowling, impatient cub.

Kaler clawed his shaggy hair away from his damp forehead before settling both fists on his hips. "That's not all. From what I could make out, she's been hit and is losing blood. A blind man could track her, and Max has better eyesight than I do."

"Will she come back here?" Leigh asked anxiously.

"Just the opposite. Her instinct will tell her to lead the enemy as far away from her baby as she can before she turns to make a stand." His jaw clenched. "Won't make much difference, though. Max can hole a quarter at two hundred yards with that Remington of his."

"Can't you stop him?"

"Not unless I can find him. Even if I do, the female will likely die anyway."

Leigh bit her lip, her protective instincts twanging like mad. "But you could try. I'll stay here with the baby and—"

"What about your father? What happens if that aneurysm bursts while you're baby-sitting?"

She winced, awash in sudden guilt. Some great daughter she was. "Then we'll just have to take Simba with us."

He looked startled before one eyebrow lifted slowly. "Simba?"

"Names are very important. They can mold a child's entire character."

She shoved the rifle at Kaler, forcing him to take it back, then jumped down and scooped the cub into her arms. Startled, the baby squirmed and hissed, and then proceeded to lick Leigh's face with a rough, wet tongue.

"Isn't he adorable, Kaler? Just like a kitten I had once."

"Give him a few more months and he'll be bigger than you are."

Laughing, she arched her head back, trying to keep from being licked to death. The sun slanted through the clearing to color her skin and coax bursts of golden fire from her hair. After the first day, she'd given up trying to smooth it into sleek sophistication and it curled in an every-which-way mop around her face.

Her shirt was already ripped by the cubs sharp little nails, and her shorts were streaked with dust from the baby's paws. Already she was treating the cub to a nonstop mixture of baby talk and stern motherly admonitions, and the crazy little creature was loving it.

The uptight career lady with the impossible standards seemed to have disappeared somewhere between Belle's place and here. He wished she hadn't. It would have made things a lot harder when he had to walk away from her.

Scowling, he gave the quiet place a last quick look, sent a silent apology to the cat whose only sin was self-preservation and then he hooked a hand under Leigh's elbow.

"C'mon, Mommy. We'd better find something for Simba to eat before he starts nibbling on your ear."

Eleven

―――――

"Okay, sport. Let's see how you do as a wet nurse."

Kaler waited while Leigh settled the cub in Daniel's lap. Then, using the tip of a knife blade, Kaler poked a tiny hole in the corner of a ZipLoc Bag filled with reconstituted powdered milk.

By this time Simba was mewing steadily, his belly obviously empty. He was too large for Daniel's lap, and his hind legs tended to dangle, annoying the hungry baby to no end.

"Whoa, hold on," Leigh admonished as the cat started to slip.

"Here, let me," the ambassador offered as he squatted next to Daniel and used his hands to support the outsize paws while Kaler showed Daniel how to use his finger to trick the cub into nursing. The baby protested a few times, shaking his head and spattering Daniel's face with drops of milk.

"See, he doesn't like that yucky milk, either!"

"Sweetheart, it's all we have," Leigh murmured, hovering anxiously.

"Give him time," Kaler added. "It just takes some creatures longer to figure out what's good for them."

Danny persisted and soon the baby was sucking contentedly, his rumbling purrs loud as a buzz saw. Kaler watched for a few seconds, then, satisfied, walked to the top of the small rise and looked around. He'd been on edge ever since they'd left the cougar's den. It wasn't anything concrete, anything he could analyze. That was the problem.

"Something tells me you've done this before," Leigh murmured by way of greeting as she came up behind him.

"Done what?"

"Rescued motherless creatures."

He shrugged. "A time or two, when I was a kid. I've never had to use a sandwich bag, though. There was always a nursing bottle at home I could filch."

"I suppose you're good at diapering, too. Babies, I mean." Her tone was rueful.

"I've done my share. Why?"

"A private bet I had with myself. I lost."

He frowned and looked as though he was going to pull her into his arms and kiss her. But they weren't alone. And from the dark frown hovering in his eyes, she had a feeling he was already working on his goodbye speech.

She plucked a spray from a nearby pine and ran her fingers over the prickly needles. Now what? she thought.

"What will you do with the cub?" she finally asked.

"Give it to a woman I know. She works with a local wildlife protection group. They'll keep him until he's ready to be on his own, and then teach him how to hunt."

"Does that always work?"

"Not always, no. But it's better than emasculating him by making him a damn pet."

She smiled, but suddenly she felt as though a great weight was crushing her. She pulled a needle from the twig and watched it fall straight as an arrow to the ground.

"I have a feeling Danny's already making plans for Simba." Plans that most definitely include you, she added silently.

Kaler glanced at the back of the boy's blond head. "I have a feeling he's not the only one thinking about Simba's future."

Leigh colored. "He *is* adorable."

"He's also a wild creature, Leigh."

"I know." She stripped off the rest of the needles and stared at the barren branch. Words had never been a problem for her before, especially when she'd told Kaler exactly what she'd thought of him and his character. She'd been so sure, so adamantly positive, that she had all the answers. Black and white, right and wrong. They were so clear, so stupidly, blindly fixed in her mind.

"I have so much to say and no way to say it." Her smile was gentle, but her eyes were shadowed. Kaler knew that look. He'd seen that same desperate emotion in his own eyes a time or two.

Regret.

He shoved his hands into his back pockets. It was harder to touch her that way. "I would be like Simba in your world, Leigh. I'd only end up fighting my way free and hurting someone in the process."

Leigh nodded, her throat threatening to close with each breath she took. It would have helped if he'd told her that he loved her. Or would it?

"Danny loves it here, and I'm getting very fond of it myself. We could visit."

"And then what? Say goodbye all over again?"

Her attempt at a smile failed miserably. "Looks like we just can't seem to get the timing right."

Leigh watched the expressions chasing across his face one by one. The sun wasn't kind to him, and his face showed every hard-lived year. And yet he was a nice man. A good man. A man who had grieved because a wild creature had had to die.

"About Dan," he said slowly. "I'd like to hear about him now and then if you don't mind."

Leigh felt something break loose inside her. "Oh, Kaler, I wish..." She let her voice trail off, too full of pain to continue.

"I know. Me too." He used his thumb to wipe a smudge of dust from her chin, left there by the cub's paw, and Leigh trembled.

He leaned forward and kissed her, his mouth warm and desperate. If only he'd said he loved her, she would have talked until she was blue in the face in an effort to change his mind. But he hadn't.

"Will you go with us to the hospital in Seattle?" she asked when he released her.

"No. Someone has to see to Simba."

Her thoughts were full of regret and love as she went onto tiptoe and pulled his head down to hers. She opened her mouth over his and kissed him with only those feelings in mind.

He reacted like a spark to dry tinder, his answering kisses heated and as hungry as only a lonely man's kisses can be. Even as he dragged her against him, her arms were seeking a stronger purchase around his neck.

He responded by kissing her with the kind of raw need he hadn't felt since he was an unskilled boy driven by emotions he hadn't begun to understand.

He kissed her throat, her scent firing a surge of memories. His tongue licked at the tiny pulse just above the gold chain circling her neck, and it leapt violently.

Using his palms, he slowly skimmed his hands down her sides, memorizing every rounded curve and sleek angle. In his mind he pictured her as she'd been on that morning outside the tent, with the sun streaking gold into her hair and her mouth eager for his. He wrenched his lips from hers and dragged her arms from his neck.

"Tonight," she whispered, her eyes afire and her mouth soft. "When Father and Daniel are asleep."

Yes! Kaler thought, his blood pooling hot and demanding at his groin. "No," he said with a rough catch in his voice. "It ends here. Now. No recriminations. No regrets."

Leigh was suddenly drowning. Somehow, though, she managed to maintain her composure. Function in adversity, finish in style. Mama would be proud, she thought as she smoothed her shirt and tried to pat her hair into place.

"Since we're tying up lose ends, please allow me to thank you for everything," she said softly. "You've been a good friend to me and to Father." Tears welled, but she kept her voice remarkably steady. "And a wonderful role model for Danny."

She made it all the way to a dark secluded grove of mountain oak before the sobs came.

"No, Simba, the trail goes this way," Daniel ordered, pulling on the strap tied to the red bandanna around the cub's sturdy neck. Instead of obeying, the tiny cougar cried shrilly, determined to head off the trail toward a tumble of boulders.

"No, Simba," the boy repeated, more harshly this time. "There's nothing over there but rocks."

Leigh smiled at her son. It had been a long afternoon for all of them. "Maybe he's hungry."

"Not again," the ambassador muttered in a low voice. His face was pale, but he seemed to be breathing easily and walking without strain. Just to make sure, however, she had stuck to his side like glue, letting Daniel walk in front of them.

"Now, Dad, he's just a baby." She glanced toward Kaler, who had taken the lead and kept it. As though he felt her eyes on him, he turned his head and met her gaze.

"Problems?"

"Simba seems to be a little rebellious."

Daniel tugged on the strap but the cougar was too strong for him and broke loose. *"Simba!"* Shouting for him to stop, Danny raced after him.

Kaler saw a blur of tan as the cub streaked toward the rocks he seemed to find so fascinating. *"Danny! Stop!"* he yelled, even as he was sprinting to catch him.

Leigh saw the wounded female cougar a second before it launched itself free of an overhanging rock toward her son. Her scream was lost in the ear-splitting snarl of the attacking cat.

Acting on instinct, Kaler tackled the cougar in midair, inadvertently sending them both crashing into the running child. Danny tumbled sideways, his head smashing against a piece of granite.

Kaler heard Leigh scream, and then he felt a rib give way as the animal struggled to free itself for another attack. He held on, his arms straining from the effort.

"Rifle!" he managed to shout, then saw that the ambassador was already aiming. But the big cat was fired by a mother's rage. Freeing a front leg, she struck viciously, her needle-sharp claws opening Kaler's chest from his shoulder to his belly button.

Kaler sucked in against the pain and, at the same time, saw Leigh crouching protectively in front of her son. If the cat got through him, she was next, and then Danny.

Gritting his teeth against the hot agony draining his strength, Kaler gouged a purchase in the hard dirt with the toes of his boots, then managed to roll to his back, taking the cat with him.

"Shoot!" he screamed, but the ambassador hesitated, the carbine's barrel trying to track the hissing, spitting cat as she fought furiously to free herself.

Kaler's grip slipped, and the cat started to scramble free. Kaler clutched a handful of fur and managed to duck a vicious, clawing jab to the face. A shot rang out, nearly deafening him. The cougar jerked, then fell heavily, pinning his arm beneath her muscular hindquarters.

"Damn it, Kale," grumbled a deep voice somewhere to his right. "Ain't you got any better sense than to take on a spitting mad cougar with your bare hands?"

It was Guntar.

"Have another belt of brandy, Bradbury. It'll do you good." Max wiped the top of the whiskey bottle with his sleeve before handing it to the ambassador.

"Hey, I'm the one in pain here," Kaler grumbled, then sucked in against the stab of agony in his ribs. A few yards away, the animal that had broken those ribs was lying dead under the tarp Max had thrown over her hours earlier.

"He's right, Max," Bradbury said in the ultraprecise tones he'd been using for the past half hour, ever since the high-test home brew had taken hold.

The Forest Service helicopter summoned by the signal fire Max had built had been too small for all of them, so the pilot had flown Danny and Leigh to Seattle first. That had been nearly four hours ago, and the three vastly different men left behind had already polished off most of Max's bottle.

Above their heads the smoke cloud formed by the green wood fire had already drifted due east. If all went according to plan, the chopper would be back any minute to pick up the ambassador and Kaler.

After that, Max was to take Simba to Cashmere and report to the co-op what had happened. At the moment, the cub was curled next to Kaler's thigh, sound asleep.

With a courtly but awkward bow, the ambassador passed Kaler the flask and watched intently while he drank. The potent stuff was liquid fire, burning all the way to his empty belly.

"Better have another swallow," Leigh's father urged. "It might be hours before the helicopter gets back here to pick us up."

"Way I see it, a man who just got done tangling with a cat deserves to get himself good and drunk," Max put in.

"Man has a point," Kaler said to the ambassador, who nodded solemnly.

"He does indeed."

"Here's to Danny," Kaler said fiercely, lifting the bottle. "He'd damn well better make it."

The boy had been conscious and moving when they'd loaded him on the chopper—both good signs, Kaler told himself one more time as he treated himself to another generous swallow of whisky.

The gouges in his chest were still oozing blood into the T-shirt Bradbury had tied around his chest as a makeshift bandage, and Kaler was feeling decidedly light-headed.

"He's a nice-looking kid, Kale," Max said as he took back the flask and greedily swallowed his share. "Looks a lot like you did when you was his age." His grin flashed yellow against his dirty whiskers. "Like me, too, come to think of it."

"Don't start, Max," Kaler warned, trying to scowl, but his mouth felt numb, and Max's face kept going in and out of focus.

"Hell, it's a damn fact, ain't it? My old man is your old man. We got the same stuff in us, you and me. You just made more of what you got than I did."

"Some folks won't agree with you there, Max." Kaler concentrated on sitting perfectly still, but the rock face behind his back seemed to be moving, and each time it moved, he hurt more.

"Some folks might just be damn snobs, too." Max thrust out his jaw and dared Leigh's father to disagree.

"Some folks might have been significantly in error, too," Bradbury enunciated meticulously.

"What the hell does that mean, 'significantly in error'?" Max demanded pugnaciously.

"It means I was wrong about this man here." Bradbury nodded in Kaler's direction, and his silver hair seemed to glint in the long rays of the afternoon sun. "I thought he would ruin my daughter's life."

"Gave it my best shot, didn't I?" Kaler muttered, grabbing the bottle again. It took two swallows before he could empty it. This time the burning stayed in his gut and sweat popped out on his forehead. After tossing aside the empty, he sucked in against the pain and wiped his face with his hand.

"She loves you, you know," Bradbury said.

"Thinks she does, you mean."

Leigh had cried when she'd kissed him goodbye before climbing aboard the chopper. And she'd made him promise not to leave the hospital until they'd talked. As if he would, he thought irritably. He had to make sure the kid was all right, didn't he?

"My grandson seems to think you're some kind of walking encyclopedia on matters of mountain lore," Bradbury persisted.

Max rubbed his jaw and frowned. "If that means that Kale here knows these parts better'n anyone, the kid's right. He does. even better'n me, if you can believe it."

"That is hard to believe," Bradbury agreed.

"I can see now why you were in the diplomatic service," Kaler muttered. To his shock, Leigh's father grinned, and for the first time Kaler saw a resemblance between father and daughter. The old bastard might not be all that bad after all.

"One thing I learned in that capacity, Mr. Kaler, was never to travel dry." He glanced toward the jumble of packs to the right. "I know it doesn't measure up to Max's firewater, but I do happen to have a pint of twelve-year-old Scotch in my pack. For medicinal purposes only, you understand."

"Hotdamn!" Max exclaimed as he scrambled to his feet and executed a clumsy bow. "Allow me to get it for you, Ambassador."

"With pleasure, Max."

Still grinning, Max walked somewhat unsteadily toward the packs. Bradbury watched briefly, then turned his shrewd blue eyes on Kaler.

"Mr. Kaler, why didn't you take the deal Stu Carlton offered you seven years ago?"

Kaler took a moment to figure out what the devil Bradbury was talking about. "Wasn't much of a deal," he muttered.

"You would have been able to keep your job and your reputation."

Kaler leaned his head against the cool granite and stared up at the lingering wisps of black smoke. "Maybe I was burned out."

"Or perhaps you didn't want to damage Leigh's career."

"Bull."

"Carlton would have had to overrule her decision to terminate you by letting you retire. You know enough about government bureaucracy to know that that would have been a serious slap in the face to Leigh."

Kaler briefly considered stonewalling the old man, then decided that it didn't matter what he did. He and Leigh had run out their string anyway.

"What the hell," he said. "I'd had my shot at Customs. It's her turn now."

Bradbury shifted his gaze toward Max, who was muttering obscenities to himself as he pulled things from the pack one by one. "Are you and Max really brothers?" he asked.

"Half brothers," Kaler said with an edge to his voice. "We had the same father."

Bradbury nodded. "I see now why you were always so defensive about your background."

"Me?"

"Yes indeed. According to Leigh, you don't think you're good enough for her, but, of course, you're wrong. You might not have the background she has, but inside, where it counts, you are a true gentleman in the best sense of the word."

"The hell I am!"

"A family tree has to start somewhere. Why not with you two and Danny?"

The thought lingered in Kaler's mind, as precious as a cooling spring rain after a seven-year drought. A man would be a fool not to want a family like that to call his own. A man would be a fool if he thought he could make it work.

"You know what, Bradbury? You're drunk, that's what you are."

"Perhaps, but I'm also a good judge of men. You're exactly what my daughter needs, to put the glow back in her eyes. And besides, if she wants you, she won't stop until she gets you."

Kaler was beginning to think he was dreaming this entire conversation. Winston Bradbury couldn't possibly be smiling at him as though he actually liked the idea.

"Found it!" Max shouted, waving the bottle in the air. Getting to his feet, he staggered slightly before catching his balance and headed back their way.

After half falling, half settling again, he twisted off the bottle cap and took the first swallow. "For services rendered," he said with a wink as he handed the bottle to the ambassador.

"To life," Bradbury said, saluting Kaler with the bottle before drinking. He passed the Scotch to Kaler, saying as he did, "you saved Daniel's life. For that, you have my gratitude and my friendship, no matter what you decide to do."

Kaler stared at the familiar label, his eyes stinging suddenly. Brushing the embossed paper with his thumb, he thought about the mixture of bitterness and desire and contentment he'd felt during the past few days. And he thought about the eagerness for living that had filled him when he'd opened his eyes to a new day and found Leigh nestled next to him.

"To life," he said in a raw tone. And to the woman I love, he added silently. God give me the strength to let her go. For her own good.

Twelve

Leigh sat stiffly, her eyes and ears focused on the double doors less than a room's length away. Behind those doors, one of Seattle General's best surgical teams had just finished removing a blood clot pressing against Danny's brain.

It had been more than six hours since they'd taken him into the OR, looking so impossibly fragile and pale on the adult-size gurney.

"Here, drink this," Kaler ordered.

Leigh glanced up and shook her head. The bulky bandage wrapping his chest showed white above the loose-fitting surgical smock the emergency surgeon had lent him, and his face seemed almost as white.

"I can't. More coffee will make me sick."

"It's chicken soup. You need it."

"No, I'm fine."

"Like hell you are! For the past hour you've been going on nerves and stubbornness." He took one of her hands and put the soup into it. "Drink."

Knowing he wouldn't sit down again until she did as he directed, she took a tiny sip. The soup was too hot and too salty, but it warmed her all the way down.

"Thanks," she murmured, waiting for him to ease his bruised and aching body into the hard waiting room chair he had left ten minutes earlier.

When the chopper had finally gotten him and the ambassador to the ER, Kaler had been exhausted and woozy from the liquor and the loss of blood. The ER doctor had sutured him and ordered him to bed. He'd put up a good fight, but the whiskey and the sedative they'd snuck into his veins along with a pint of blood had put him down for the count.

He had slept off the sedative and then, when he'd come to again, he'd removed the IV attached to his arm and gone looking for Leigh.

He'd found her in the OR waiting room, looking lost and breakable and yet as fiercely protective of her baby as the now-dead mama cougar had been.

"Any news?" he asked, his gaze, too, going repeatedly to the two doors.

Leigh shook her head. "He's still in recovery. The doctor said he came through surgery fine—no complications—but he's still out."

"It's the best thing for him right now. He'll wake up when he's ready."

Because he was watching, she managed another quick sip. "Did you see Father?"

"Yeah, the nurse said he won't wake up for hours yet."

As soon as he'd arrived at Seattle General and learned that his grandson had been scheduled for brain surgery, the ambassador's blood pressure had gone dangerously high, and the neurosurgeon had ordered up a bed and twenty-four hours of rest.

"What about the aneurysm?"

"He's scheduled for tests first thing tomorrow morning."

"At least he's here."

"Don't worry, Leigh. Unless I'm dead wrong about the man, he plans to live a lot of years yet."

A middle-aged African-American nurse in green scrubs walked by, and Leigh hailed her eagerly. "Mrs. Williams, can I see my son now?"

"Not yet, Mrs. Bradbury. Danny's still in recovery, but he's doing just fine. I'll come and get you as soon as he's moved to his room."

"Thank you."

The nurse nodded and disappeared behind the doors.

Leigh drew a long breath and told herself to be patient. "Danny's never been in a hospital since he was born. He'll be so scared if he wakes up and I'm not there."

Kaler took her free hand in his. Her fingers were icy and curled desperately around his. "He's a scrapper, like his mom. He'll make it."

"You're bleeding again," Leigh murmured, her gaze resting on the thick bandage.

Kaler shrugged, then held his breath against the wave of pain threatening to push him into unconsciousness again.

"I'm a big guy," he said when the pain eased marginally. "I can stand to lose a pint or two." He sat stiffly, his movements restricted by the two broken ribs, a sprained right wrist and more than a hundred sutures in his chest.

"You saved Danny's life."

Kaler scowled. "I knocked him into that damn rock is what I did." The guilt was still heavy inside him, hurting far worse than his busted ribs.

"If you hadn't..." Leigh pictured the cougar's needle-sharp claws ripping into Danny's small chest and she shuddered. "You told me to leave the cub alone. I didn't listen." Her lips were bloodless and scarcely moved as she spoke. "I never listen."

Her fingers threatened to crush the foam cup, and Kaler plucked it free before the hot soup ended up in her lap. He headed for a trash receptacle a dozen paces farther down the corridor, not far by mountain standards, but far enough for a man whose every breath threatened to tear something loose inside.

"You never let anyone help you, do you?" she grated when he finally made it back to his chair in one piece.

"Isn't that a case of the pot and the kettle, Hank?" he chided as he eased into the chair again. It was made for a midget or a contortionist, he decided, but not for a guy of normal height and weight.

"Are you sure you trust Max to take Simba to your friend, the animal lady?"

"No, but I trust the pilot to relay my message to Rusty. She'll watch Max like a hawk."

"I feel so sorry for that mama cougar, but I know how she felt when she thought her baby needed her."

Her eyes were bloodshot from lack of sleep, and her hair was a frizzled disaster. It occurred to him that he had never seen her look more beautiful. He took her hand again and rested it under his on his thigh.

"It's nature's way, Leigh."

"I was so sure I was doing the right thing...." Her gaze dropped, and Kaler felt her hand tremble under his. "I know this isn't the right time, and there's really no way I can make this easy, but there's something you have to know, something I should have told you before now." She stopped and drew a shaky breath. "Danny's not really six and a half. He's only five, and he's not your son. I...I lied to get you to help me."

It took everything she had left to turn and face his contempt. Instead, she saw a tender smile in his eyes.

"I'm—why aren't you yelling at me and calling me all the names I called you?"

"Not my style, I guess."

"But I deliberately lied. I... used you." The throbbing ache in her voice made him regret every bitter thought he'd had during the past few days.

"I know that, Hank. I've known from the beginning. I just needed you to tell me the truth on your own."

Leigh blinked, then realized that she was suddenly very, very cold inside. "How could you possibly know?"

Kaler realized that he'd never told anyone else what he was about to tell her. Perhaps because he'd never quite come to terms with the implications before. Just thinking about it was making his face hot and his skin clammy.

"It's not easy for me to admit this, but I came on so strong to you about not wanting children because I couldn't give you a child, even if you'd begged me. I've been sterile since Nam. Infection. It's permanent and irreversible."

Leigh felt something break loose inside her. "But...if you knew I was lying, why did you let me get away with it?"

"Because I couldn't blame you for protecting your child any more than I can blame that mother cougar. And because you needed me."

Tears flooded her eyes, blurring his face. Her fingers were numb where his clutched hers. "I still need you," she whispered brokenly. "Only you don't need me."

Kaler couldn't quite keep his gaze steady on hers and shifted it to the wall next to her. "I need you, but a man has to have more to offer a woman than his need. There isn't a thing I can give you that you don't already have. Not even a child."

"What about a little down-to-earth humor when I'm taking myself too seriously, and a broad shoulder to lean on when life gets too scary?" she suggested softly, drawing his gaze again. Her glance dropped pointedly to the big hand enveloping hers. "And a big strong hand to hold when I'm feeling weak and helpless inside?"

He turned his hand so that hers was balanced on his. "That's not enough—"

"I married Edward because he'd been in love with me since we were both sixteen and I was feeling lost and alone. He was rich and wellborn and a genuinely nice guy. He had three degrees and a successful law practice. His roots were sunk even deeper into the Old South than mine. As you said once, the perfect match. But after he was gone and the loneliness set in again, it was you I found myself missing, you I wanted to be holding me at night. I still do, and if you walk away again, it'll break my heart."

His face went very still, and his fingers curled painfully around hers. "Did anyone ever tell you that you play dirty?"

In spite of the worry and weariness in her eyes, they sparkled for an instant before she said softly, "Games are for kids who have time to play them. I don't."

Kaler realized that he couldn't think of even one more objection. He couldn't seem to think of anything but Leigh and the little boy they were waiting to see.

From somewhere close came the sound of three quiet bongs, followed by a melodious voice paging the radiologist on call. Leigh's gaze whipped to the double doors again, just in time to see the nurse emerging. This time she was grinning.

"Good news. Danny's awake and asking for you. Give us ten minutes to get him settled in his room and then come on up. It's 624, in the south wing."

Leigh's fingernails dug into Kaler's hand. "Is he all right?"

"He's fine. In fact, he's hungry. Wants me to sneak him in some Snickers bars, and I might just do that." She shifted her gaze to Kaler, and her grin widened. "Your son is a born charmer."

Kaler had trouble with his throat. It seemed to be clogged with something thick. "Probably'll run us ragged by the time he's ten," he said in a graveled tone.

"Count on it," the nurse said before she slipped back behind the doors.

Leigh's heart was suddenly racing. "I have a witness," she said through her tears.

"It's a hell of a long shot, you and me," he warned. "I'm used to living alone, I refuse to shave in winter even under pain of torture and I'm a total bust at cocktail parties."

"Duly noted."

"I won't leave the mountains. It's where I belong now."

"I'll find a job here, with Customs, if I can. If not, I'm just egotistical enough to believe I can find something else. Who knows? Maybe the two of us can start our own wildlife protection agency, or I can come along on your fishing parties and do the cooking."

Tears were streaming down her face, and he wiped them away with fingers that weren't as steady as they should be.

"What about Dan? He might not like the idea of taking on a new dad, especially me."

"Let's go ask him." Leigh got to her feet, then used both her hands to help him get to his. Fiery pain shot through him, making him light-headed. Leigh slipped a shoulder under his arm and held on, supporting him until his head cleared.

"What if he says no?" he said when he could breathe again.

"He won't. He's got his mother's genes, remember? He likes a challenge." She arched upward to kiss him gently on the cheek. "And you, my darling husband-to-be, are definitely a challenge."

Kaler felt a moment of happiness so intense, it nearly staggered him. But a man kept his emotions to himself. Didn't he? Sure he did, he thought. Except when Leigh was looking up at him with a world of promises in her soft brown eyes.

"There are conditions to this arrangement," he said gruffly, knowing that he was fast losing ground.

Her mouth trembled at the memory of that morning only six days and a lifetime ago. "What conditions?"

"As soon as we're married, you and Danny are going to have my name and no one else's."

"Agreed. What next?"

"You have to promise never to make coffee for me again."

Leigh's jaw dropped, and Kaler chuckled. "I love you more than my life, Leigh Bradbury, but your coffee tastes like river silt."

Leigh felt her world tilt and then right itself. Someday he would be able to say those words baldly, without self-consciously slipping them in as an aside. She would see to that, even if it took her a lifetime.

"I wouldn't talk, if I were you," she said, wanting to shout with happiness. Her son was going to be all right, and the man she loved had just told her that he loved her, too. "My poor stomach is still trying to digest those eggs à la Kaler."

Kaler watched her lips curve into a teasing pout, and for a moment he couldn't say another word. "I think I've just made a big mistake here. How the hell can I be so crazy about a woman who doesn't appreciate my talents?"

Leigh burst out laughing. "Come on, Daddy. Let's go see our son. And then I'll do my best to show you which of your talents I *do* appreciate."

"Bossing me around again, are you?"

"Absolutely. Any objections?"

Kaler tried, but he couldn't think of a single one. So he kissed her instead.

* * * * *

It's Opening Night in October—
and you're invited!
Take a look at romance with a
brand-new twist, as the stars
of tomorrow make their
debut today!
It's LOVE:
an age-old story—
now, with
*WORLD PREMIERE
APPEARANCES* by:

Patricia Thayer—Silhouette Romance #895
JUST MAGGIE—Meet the Texas rancher who wins this pretty
teacher's heart…and lose your own heart, too!

Anne Marie Winston—Silhouette Desire #742
BEST KEPT SECRETS—Join old lovers reunited and see what
secret wonders have been hiding…beneath the flames!

Sierra Rydell—Silhouette Special Edition #772
ON MIDDLE GROUND—Drift toward Twilight, Alaska, with this
widowed mother and collide—heart first—into body heat
enough to melt the frozen tundra!

Kate Carlton—Silhouette Intimate Moments #454
KIDNAPPED!—Dare to look on as a timid wallflower blos-
soms and falls in fearless love—with her gruff, mysterious
kidnapper!

**Don't miss the classics of tomorrow—
premiering today—only from**

In the spirit of Christmas, Silhouette invites
you to share the joy of the holiday season.

Experience the beauty of Yuletide romance with Silhouette
Christmas Stories 1992—a collection of heartwarming stories by
favorite Silhouette authors.

JONI'S MAGIC by Mary Lynn Baxter
HEARTS OF HOPE by Sondra Stanford
THE NIGHT SANTA CLAUS RETURNED by Marie Ferrarella
BASKET OF LOVE by Jeanne Stephens

This Christmas you can also receive a FREE keepsake Christmas
ornament. Look for details in all November and December
Silhouette books.

Also available this year are three popular early editions of
Silhouette Christmas Stories—1986, 1987 and 1988. Look for these
and you'll be well on your way to a complete collection of the
best in holiday romance.

Share in the celebration—with Silhouette's
Christmas gift of love.

SX92

TAKE A WALK ON THE DARK SIDE OF LOVE

October is the shivery season, when chill winds blow and shadows walk the night. Come along with us into a haunting world where love and danger go hand in hand, where passions will thrill you and dangers will chill you. Come with us to

In this newest short story collection from Silhouette Books, three of your favorite authors tell tales just perfect for a spooky autumn night. Let Anne Stuart introduce you to "The Monster in the Closet," Helen R. Myers bewitch you with "Seawitch," and Heather Graham Pozzessere entice you with "Wilde Imaginings."

Silhouette Shadows™
Haunting a store near you this October.

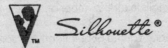